James Henry Salisbury

Original Investigations in Diphtheria and Scarlet Fever

showing their kinship and cause to be the Mucor malignans - a fungus in

the exudations, blood, urine and sputa

James Henry Salisbury

Original Investigations in Diphtheria and Scarlet Fever
showing their kinship and cause to be the Mucor malignans - a fungus in the exudations, blood, urine and sputa

ISBN/EAN: 9783337392734

Printed in Europe, USA, Canada, Australia, Japan

Cover: Foto ©Andreas Hilbeck / pixelio.de

More available books at **www.hansebooks.com**

IN

DIPHTHERIA AND SCARLET FEVER,

SHOWING THEIR KINSHIP AND CAUSE TO BE THE

MUCOR MALIGNANS,

(A Fungus in the Exudations, Blood, Urine and Sputa,)

*CURED BY QUININE TOPICALLY ADMINISTERED IN POWDER ON THE TONGUE,
AND BY INHALATION.*

BY

JAMES H. SALISBURY, B. N. S., A. M., M. D.,

MEMBER PHILOSOPHICAL SOCIETY OF GREAT BRITAIN, OF AMERICAN ANTIQUARIAN SOCIETY, AMERICAN ASSOCIATION FOR THE
ADVANCMENT OF SCIENCE, VICE-PRESIDENT WESTERN RESERVE HISTORICAL SOCIETY, AUTHOR PRIZE ESSAY ON
MALARIA, 1882, AND OF PUBLISHED AND UNPUBLISHED WORKS AND PAPERS.

DIPHTHERIA AND SCARLET FEVER.

(*Reprinted from "Gaillard's Medical Journal."*)

DIPHTHERIA AND SCARLET FEVER, BY JAMES H. SALISBURY, B. N. S., A. M., M. D., New York : 1882. (*All rights reserved.*)

Microscopical investigations connected with the exudation and expectoration of angina membranacea, angina maligna or gangrenosa, and scarlatina anginosa; resulting in the discovery of the source of and the pathological process by which the exudations are produced, and the further discovery of a peculiar species of Mucor developing in the diphtheritic membranes of angina maligna and which appears to be the true cause of the disease ; with some remarks on treatment.

Also some general conclusions on the ætiology of fevers; the peculiar functions of the epithelial systemic cell envelope; and the probable way in which the system receives a more or less permanent protective immunity, by one attack of certain contagious diseases against a second invasion of the same.

M. Bretonneau gave to angina membranacea the name of diphtheritis, on account of the pellicle-like exudations. The ordinary sites of these exudations, as is well known, are the fauces and pharynx; often however they extend past the pharyngeal and laryngeal regions far down the œsophagus, and into the trachea and bronchial tubes, and even upward into the nasal fossæ.

Microscopic examinations show, further, that there is a tendency also for the lining membranes of the genital organs, intestines and bladder, and in short the epithelial cells of the entire mucous surface to take on the diphtheritic action. This renders it evident that this disease, like scarlatina anginosa, (which it will be shown to resemble) is systemic, with a marked tendency to localization in the respiratory tract.

Angina maligna, in its worst form, accompanied by angina membranacea, became epidemic during the months of October, November and December of the year 1862, and January and February, 1863, over a tract of country, about five miles long from north-west to south-east, and three miles wide, situated from two and a half to five miles south-west and west of the city of Lancaster, Ohio.

It first appeared immediately after a snow storm (the first of the season in October). The snow fell about two inches deep, upon a remarkably dry, parched soil, and was the beginning of the fall wet weather, after a long period of drought, which was so severe that it was impossible for the farmers to plow their soil, for putting in the winter wheat. The grasses of pastures and meadows were parched, dry, and mostly dead; and the herbaceous plants of the fields and forests were in the same condition. The disease first made its appearance at the south-east end of the section before described, among the dry sandy hills, and gradually progressed to the north-west. It exhibited, often in the same family, all grades of severity from a mild type of *angina membranacea* to the most severe form of *angina maligna*; where the extremities would become gangrenous, in some cases, several days before death. The malignant form

401

was unusually fatal and rapid in its progress; often from two to five persons dying in a single family, within a few days of each other. The young became the victims; while those above twenty-five usually escaped.

The section over which this malignant disease prevailed, composed of hills and high table lands, is abundantly supplied with fine springs of cold, free stone water, and is regarded as a particularly healthy region. It is inhabited mostly by sober, industrious German farmers.

An excellent opportunity was here offered for studying the disease. Through the kindness of Doctors Effinger, Boerstler and Lewis I was able to obtain the best of material for examination.

From its progress in this region, from family to family, and from other circumstances, hereafter mentioned, there appeared to be no doubt of its contagious character. The period of incubation ranged, in different cases, from three to six and eight days; unless, accidentally, the air passages became directly inoculated with the virus or vegetation, in which case, the disease would begin to show itself immediately.

The cases could be nearly all traced to exposure to the contagion of the disease. When it once made its appearance in a family, any of the younger members seldom escaped.

Before entering upon a description of the following cases, and the microscopic examinations of the exudations, etc., I will briefly narrate the characters of angina membranacea and angina maligna, set forth by Dr. Tweedie; as his remarks upon these diseases, in several important particulars, point in the direction of the results of these investigations.

In speaking of angina membranacea, he says: "The patches are of various extent; in mild cases, white and ashy, separate, and presenting the appearance of superficial sloughs, for which they have often been mistaken; in others, dark colored, coalescent, and forming one uniform crust. The exudations may extend far down the

œsophagus, or into the larynx, trachea and bronchiæ, and upward into the nasal fossæ. The membrane beneath and between the pellicles is in some cases of a bright red, and in others purplish or livid. The exudations vary in density, from that of coagulable lymph, to that of soft pultaceous matter."

" The local sensations are similar to those of angina diffusa, with the addition of that produced by irritation and obstruction of the air passages, when the disease has extended in that direction. It is common also for the sub-maxillary and cervical glands to become inflamed and tumefied.

"The general symptoms are those of fever, and vary with the type of the latter and the degree of the inflammation. Where the patches are but few and circumscribed, the disease is often called *ulcerated sore throat*, such as may be seen in *scarlatina anginosa*, but there are no ulcers in these cases, for on removing the pellicles or sloughs, as they are called, we find the membrane beneath quite free from any other disorganization than the loss of its epithelium. In the worst cases, the pellicles are discolored by the admixture of bloody exudation and vitiated secretions of the throat, so as to create an impression that the parts are in a state of *sphacelus*.

"These casts correspond to the *angina maligna* of others; but we have the united testimony of Bretonneau, Guersent, and Deslandes, formed on extensive microscopic observations, that there are no true eschars in these cases. The idea of gangrene existing has been further kept up by the discharge of serous and fetid matter from the nostrils, and by the putrid character of the fever. Instances of this description are very rarely met with, excepting when the disease prevails as an epidemic.

"From the above, it appears that angina membranacea occurs in two forms. In one the local affection bears the marks of active inflammation, in the bright hue of the mucous membrane, and in the white, circumscribed exudations, unmixed with blood or sanies.

" The constitutional symptoms in this form are likewise sthenic, the pulse being full and firm, the skin warm, and the nervous system—though disturbed—not exhibiting the prostration so common in *typhoid forms.* The other variety may well be called *angin maligna.*

"Its approach is often insidious, being attended with little pain or disturbance in the throat till the false membrane is already extensively formed, then the dysphagia becomes extreme ; liquids are forced back through the nostrils, and symptoms soon occur denoting that the air passages are obstructed ; such as a croupy cough, hoarseness, and stridulous breathing.

" The feeling of suffocation accompanying these symptoms, is in part owing to the swelling of the lymphatic glands. On inspection of the throat, we see a thick pellicle, sometimes dense, not unfrequently pultaceous, variously colored, according to the degree of its decomposition, or to the accompanying secretions, and either continuous or interrupted by fissures which exhibit the livid hue of the membrane beneath. The pulse is extremely rapid and feeble, delirium sets in early, and is soon followed by coma ; and the collapsed face and sunken eyes indicate extreme exhaustion. Death often takes place suddenly from the laryngeal complication.

"Bretonneau was led by the results of his dissections, to attribute the death, in all the fatal cases, to the changes in the air passages.

"As might be expected, *a priori*, the victims of *malignant angina*, are persons living in humid districts, where the disease is occasionally epidemic ; among the inhabitants of crowded buildings, and the poor ill-fed classes of the community.

"Persons, however, not under these depressing agencies, may be attacked by a severe form of the disease. *Children are more liable to it than adults.* Whether it is propagated by contagion is not absolutely determined, but there are strong presumptions in favor of this view. When the affection is epidemic, the difficulty of distinguishing the operation of some generally diffused cause from that of contagion, meets us in this disease with the same force as in other epidemic maladies. The most unexceptionable instances of contagion are those in which the sporadic form has been transmitted from one person to another. Guersent relates the case of a nun who caught the disease from a little girl whom she had nursed in the Hôpital des Enfans, and he remarks that practitioners are frequently attacked after inspecting the throats of their patients. That the inflammation of the mucous membrane takes place in angina membranacea cannot be denied, but why it should cause the secretion of coagulable lymph, rather than of serum and mucus, which are the ordinary products of mucous inflammation, cannot easily be explained. It is probable, however, that the peculiarity does not depend upon the local action merely, but upon the state of the constitution previously modified by epidemic influence.

"In this disease there is frequently observed an erythematous or papular eruption on different parts of the body, and there can be little difficulty in arriving at the conclusion that it is a variety of *scarlatina maligna.*"

Dr. Tweedie further says: "We are inclined to affirm that *scarlatina simplex*, *scarlatina anginosa* and the *scarlatina* or *angina maligna*, and the sore throat, without efflorescence on the skin, are merely varieties of one and the same disease."

REPORT OF CASES.

The following communication contains a report of several well-marked cases of angina maligna which were attended and reported by Dr Effinger:

DEAR DOCTOR: At your request, I have kept a careful record of the following well-marked cases of *angina maligna*, from which I have sent you, from time to time, as the disease progressed, samples of blood, urine, exudations and sloughs.

CASE I.—Amos Bear, a strong, healthy young man, aged seventeen, was taken down December 4th, 1862.

Thursday morning, December 4th, he felt so badly that he remained in bed and ate no breakfast or dinner. Towards evening he vomited, felt pain in throat, neck swelling rapidly, externally. Sent for me about dark; could not see him that evening; prescribed a cathartic and foot bath, and flannel cloths wrung out of hot vinegar and sprinkled with salt, to be applied about the neck.

Friday, 10 A. M., Dec. 5th, made my first visit; found him in bed, face anxious and look depressed; pulse 92; not much fever or heat of skin; back and side of neck much swollen; more œdematous than glandular.

On examination of throat, discovered a large diphtheritic patch, one inch in diameter and oval in shape, on left tonsil. It had a dark, ashy appearance, was of soft consistence and easily penetrated, with well-defined edges; breath offensive, with a sickly meatish smell. The right side of the throat was deeply infected, engorged to a purplish hue, with a slight bloody exudation from a small surface posterior to the tonsil. Continued external applications, and left chlorate of potash to be taken internally every four hours and used as a gargle.

Saturday, 12 M., Dec. 6th.—Pulse 92. General symptoms same as yesterday; no change in slough on left side; some lumps of putrid matter, separated with difficulty by a spoon-handle; fetor of breath more decidedly putrid than before. On the right tonsil, a well-defined diphtheritic exudation had made its appearance, three-fourths of an inch in diameter, closely adherent, but the edges could be slightly raised. The purplish engorgement not quite so distinct as yesterday. Continued treatment, with addition of mur. tinct. iron, and a more liberal diet.

Sunday, 1 P. M., Dec. 7th.—Patient not so well; had a bad night; forehead hot, pulse 92; more lassitude than before. Fetor of breath intolerable, decidedly putrid. Slough on left side about the same; dark fetid shreds removed, showing considerable depth of slough. On the right side, the diphtheritic patch was much increased in size, oblong in shape, extending below the tonsil as far as could be seen. It is much thicker than yesterday, of a whitish yellow color and more adherent. The mucous membrane on its edge still of a dark, livid color; obtained a sample of his morning urine, and the hawking expectoration produced by my examination, which I sent you. Applied wash of nitric acid, diluted two-thirds, freely, to both sides; general treatment continued, with iron omitted.

Monday, 4 P. M., Dec. 8th.—Had a very comfortable night; feels better; pulse 86; no heat of skin; fetor of breath not so offensive; slough on left side evidently arrested; dead lumps easily detached. On the right side, the tripe-looking membrane has extended over the dark, livid border of yesterday.

It now has an oval shape, and is larger than the slough opposite; its lower edge well defined a short space below tonsil. Edges closely adherent; cannot yet be detached by gentle force. Took from arm 1½ ounces of blood for examination, which I sent you, with some sloughs from fauces and a sample of his morning urine. Applied freely the nitric acid, and commenced the iron again.

Tuesday noon, Dec. 9th.—Amos not so well to-day; pulse 100; forehead too warm; neck still much swollen in front, as well as on sides; pulse rapid, feeble, and not of much force; poison evidently telling on the general system; throat same as yesterday, except on the right side, where, under the diphtheritic exudation, there is apparently a large slough; tried to separate it, but the least touch made the exposed surface bleed, and I discontinued my efforts. After a slight laxative, bowels being constipated, ordered quinine and iron, with nourishing food. I used no topical applications, except chlorinated soda and potash.

Wednesday, 12 M., Dec. 10.—Amos has less fever; pulse 92 and feeble; face haggard, and I do not like the expression of his eyes; continued the quinine and mur.

tinct. iron, with liberal diet. The slough on left side is clearing somewhat, but still looks badly. The left side is perfectly foul and ragged. I detached a portion that was loose, which I sent you in the bottle, I believe, on Saturday. I detached a few shreds from this side, and sent them to you between glass slides. You can readily distinguish them by their dirty-white appearance and tripe - like consistence, being tougher than the porous soft lumps from the left side. In the bottle you will also find some soft matter that I scooped with a spoon-handle from immediately under the exudated membrane.

Thursday, 3 P. M., Dec. 11th.—Amos has had a bad night. The diphtheritic exudation has appeared on uvula and palatine arch, on the right side. They are much swollen, and render deglutition very difficult. He drinks with great difficulty even water; most of it comes back through his nose.

It is evidently spreading upward, and is in the nasal fossæ. No difficulty yet in breathing. I obtained his morning urine and some expectoration, and matter from throat, which I sent you. I also sent you a large bottle of water from the Bear Spring. Pulse 96 and feeble.

Friday noon, Dec. 12th.—Amos is worse, prostration more apparent; difficulty of swallowing increased; the respiration more labored, and I fear the diphtheritic exudation has reached the bronchi; pulse 100, and feeble. The diphtheritic membrane is covering the velum palati and the arches to-day, for the first time.

I penciled the edge with nitrate of silver, hoping to arrest the spreading. Neck, back of ears, and half way down very much swollen, and just above the sternum very œdematous.

Saturday 10 A. M., Dec. 13th.—The diphtheritic exudation has traveled beyond the penciled caustic mark.

The specimen I send you to-day speaks for itself. You see the dark line; all beyond has spread since yesterday noon.

This specimen was taken from the uvula.

Amos is sinking; respiration still more labored, and deglutition impossible. You can hear his laborious breathing all through the house. Under the separated exudation from the uvula, there is no slough, simply a raw bleeding surface. The swelling of the neck noticed yesterday has to-day almost entirely disappeared

Sunday 10 A. M., Dec. 14th.—Amos is still living, respiration becoming more and more difficult. Asphyxia is creeping on slowly but surely. Obtained a sample of morning urine which I sent you.

Monday, Dec. 15th.—Amos died at 1 P.M. Death painful. Died of suffocation. Exudation extends into bronchi, and probably into pulmonary air cells.

CASE II.—Nancy Bear, sister of Amos, aged 21. For some months prior to her brother's illness, Nancy was absent from home, visiting relatives, some twenty miles distant. On Saturday, Dec. 13th, the family sent for her, and she came home on horseback, the evening of the same day. Though much fatigued, she hung over her gasping brother that whole night. She was constantly about him till he died, giving way very much to her feelings. She became completely prostrated on Monday; fainted at the church on Tuesday morning at the funeral, and had to be carried home. I was sent for Tuesday afternoon.

Nancy is a heavy, thick-set girl of leuco-lymphatic temperament; general health good. I saw her about dusk. Found her nervous and prostrated, but with no tangible disease, except a severe coryza affecting nasal cavities and frontal sinus. I advised salt water pediluvium, and a cathartic at bed time.

Wednesday, Dec. 17th.—Was called again to see her. Complained of soreness about the neck and throat. Both nostrils were completely stuffed up with ropy mucus, and the throat so filled as to interfere with the examination of parts, but being removed, no sign was seen of diphtheritic exudation; but the next day, Dec. 18, after a careful swabbing out of the throat, I detected a slight pearly exudation on the left tonsil.

Friday, Dec. 19th.—The symptoms about the same as yesterday.

Saturday, Dec. 20th.—Was much improved, the nasal catarrh being the prominent symptom, and the white adherent exudation not increasing. Nancy was sitting up, was cheerful, and said she was much better.

Her beau called to see her as usual, Saturday night, and she imprudently remained up with him most of the night.

Sunday, Dec. 21st.—Was sent for. Found her much worse, the tonsils and velum were swollen and red, swallowing difficult, the voice hoarse and the breathing labored and painful. Auscultation of left lung gave the sibillant rhonchus. Clearly was it evident that the catarrh of the nasal passages had crept down into the trachea and lungs, and that the whole mucous membrane of the air passages was now involved. Still there was no increase of exudation in the throat beyond the slight patch on the left tonsil.

Monday, Dec. 22nd.—Had a restless night. On raising the velum, evidence of diphtheritic patches were seen on the fauces, high up. The nostrils were filled with membrane, but not easily detached.

Tuesday, Dec. 23rd.—With my polypus forceps, I detached specimens, from both nostrils, one-eighth of an inch thick, which I sent you. In the throat it was only too apparent, both in fauces and on tonsils; in appearance, white, glossy, thin and closely adherent, but in patches. It never became continuous though she lived for a week longer.

Wednesday.—Disease gradually progressing.

Thursday, Dec. 25th.—Obtained some blood from Nancy's arm; the blood flowed directly into the smaller bottle. The blood, in larger bottle flowed into a saucer, and after standing for a short time, was poured into the bottle. Obtained also some membrane from throat and nose, with some freshly expectorated mucus, which was sent to you.

Friday, Dec. 26th.—Nancy is about the same as yesterday.

Saturday, Dec. 27th.—Nancy appears to be improving and there is some hope that she may recover.

Sunday, Dec. 28th.—Worse than yesterday; very weak; breathing labored, and pulse rapid and feeble. The exudations have extended into the tracheal and bronchial passages. From this time, the breathing grew more and more labored, until she died asphyxiated, like her brother Amos, on the night of January 1st, 1863.

CASE III.—Jesse Bear, brother of Nancy, a fine healthy boy, aged 8 years was taken down Dec. 22nd, '62.

Dec. 25th.—Jesse very sick, has a large diphtheritic exudation on each tonsil.

Dec. 27th.—Large and extensive exudations, but very little constitutional disturbance. Obtained his morning urine and some of his expectoration, which I sent you. Jesse continued to fail and the exudation to pass lower and lower into the trachea and bronchi, till, on January 6th, he expired as did his brother Amos.

CASE IV.—Peter Bear, brother of Jesse, a strong healthy boy of 12 years, was taken down with the disease, Dec. 25.

Dec. 27.—Fever very high; exudation on right tonsil; vomited while I was penciling his throat; a sample of vomited matter I sent you; Peter's case was one of simple angina membranacea and did not terminate fatally. There were three other cases in this family. Mrs. Bear, who had a slight attack; Susan, a young daughter, and a little grand-daughter, all of whom recovered. The only persons escaping were Mr. Bear, and his eldest son aged about 23.

Yours, truly,
                                    M. EFFINGER.
Dr. J. H. Salisbury.

From Dr. Effinger's report it will be seen that out of seven cases in the Bear family, three died and four recovered. In almost every instance, when malignant diphtheria (*angina maligna*) appeared in a family, it was equally, if not more fatal. In support of this fact, we will mention briefly the following instances:

Mr. Bailor had six children, and one grandchild, all of whom had diphtheria. Four died, and three recovered. Of the four that died, three were female, and one male; they were respectively three weeks, seven, eleven and twenty years of · age. Of those that recovered, one was the married daughter who had but a mild attack of angina membranacea. The ages of the two others were respectively thirteen and fifteen years. Of the daughter aged eleven, who died, one leg became gangrenous to the knee several days before death. One foot of the boy aged 7 was very much swollen and also finally became gangrenous before death.

Dr. Lewis attended this family. In the Sandris family the mother and all the children, six in number, had the disease. The mother and four of the children died, so that out of seven cases in this family, only two recovered.

In Mr. Karn's family out of four children that had the disease three died. Their ages were respectively five, eleven and fourteen. A grown daughter, aged about twenty-one, and a nursing infant escaped without taking the disease. Dr. Lewis attended this family. In two of these cases, the feet and legs up to the knees became pulseless and cold twenty-four hours before death, and there was a disposition to gangrene.

In the Brooks family, all of his children, three in number, had the disease, two recovered and one died. In Warren Stripes' family, two grown daughters, the only children at home, had the disease. One recovered and one died. The first one taken down, four or five days previous to the attack, visited Mr. Bailor's family, and helped to "lay out" one of his children that had died of the disease. In Mr. Himes's family the mother and one child only had the disease. The former recovered and the latter died.

In Mr. McCabe's family, all the children, six in number, had the disease, and all recovered.

From the foregoing statements, it will be seen that out of thirty-eight cases, there were eighteen deaths, and twenty recoveries Many of those that recovered, had merely the membranous type of the disease. This however will represent about a fair average proportion of the recoveries and deaths in those attacked with the disease, in the district previously mentioned, where malignant diphtheria prevailed. But few families in the district were exempt from the invasion,

Since writing the foregoing, I have received the following letter from Dr. Lewis, in which are reported two interesting cases of *angina maligna* or *gangrenosa*.

LANCASTER, O., April 3d, 1863.

DR. SALISBURY—DEAR SIR: Your letter asking for a report of cases of diphtheria has been received. In referring to my notes of cases, I find that the epidemic which ravaged the south-west part of our county, made its advent on the 19th day of October, 1862. Two children were attacked simultaneously in the same family, one aged nine and the other eleven years, one male and the other female. These cases had progressed for four days, before I was called to see them. I cannot, from personal observation, state the mode of the attack, but at my first visit I found the eldest (a girl), with a quick, feeble pulse, cold extremities; shrunken, pale and agonized countenance; unable to articulate; the parotid and submaxillary glands enlarged; the tonsils enlarged; the uvula elongated and of an ashy appearance; the tonsils on the right side covered with a dark fetid slough, surrounding which was an areola of an ashy appearance, beyond which the parts presented a dark cherry color, gradually disappearing. The case terminated fatally in about six hours after I saw her.

The boy was in about the same condition, but had a less aggravated form of the disease. He recovered. These two cases appeared to be the nucleus from which the disease spread; mostly in a north-west direction, choosing the slopes of the hills and high table lands, rather than the summits and valleys. This disease in its progress presented two distinct forms; the first, and most usual, was what I have termed the malignant or typhoid. This form was ushered in by a low, quick pulse, a dry harsh condition of the skin, a feeling of fulness and uneasiness in the head (not amounting to headache) dry tongue, great thirst, the parotids and glands of the neck on about the second day becoming sore to the touch, the muscles of the neck at the same time becoming stiff, the tonsils, pharynx and uvula assuming a dark cherry or purple hue. In from six to twelve hours, a small yellowish-gray spot would make its appearance upon one or both tonsils, about the size of a grain of wheat. This spot had the appearance of an erysipelatous blister, which would spread rapidly and burrow deeply, assuming a dark-brown or black hue, and forming in a few hours a fetid slough, which would, in the course of from thirty-six to forty-eight hours, begin to break down.

The condition of the skin remaining the same, the pulse becoming weaker, the strength failing rapidly, the pupil of the eye enlarged and vision partially lost, so that small objects could not be seen, and the disease often terminating fatally in from four to seven days.

The other form I have taken the liberty of calling the inflammatory, to distinguish it from the typhoid form; its mode of attack being entirely different. Coming on with full, hard, bounding pulse, congested state of the capillaries, high fever, headache, nausea, sometimes vomiting, the tongue coated with dark-brown fur, the throat assuming a clean bright scarlet hue, the exudation making its appearance about the second day, and having the appearance of milk curd of a clear white cheesy character, easily broken down. This form was readily amenable to the ordinary treatment. No death occurred from such attacks, in my practice, which during the winter was extensive, for I treated over one hundred cases from October, 1862, to February, 1863. A more detailed account of the following cases may be of interest :

CASE 1.—Aged 11. Attacked Nov. 6th,

and, from all I could learn, it appeared to be at first a mild form of the malignant type of the disease. I did not see the case till some four weeks after the attack. This with the succeeding case (2), was of much interest. The child was laboring under a low grade of fever, dry, husky skin, loss of appetite, partial vision, tenderness of abdomen, periods of intense suffering occurring every two, three or four hours, which he attributed to a sore on his foot from which the skin had been rubbed by the shoe. Upon examining the sore, I found the extremity cold, the ulcer about the size of a dime, with a shrivelled bluish elevated border, the centre of a dark fetid slough, without any appearance of granulations, having much the appearance of a chancre. The ulcer continued to increase in size, the foot assuming a mottled appearance. Soon the toes began to shrivel about the nails, dry gangrene made its appearance, soon invading the whole foot ; the brain became implicated, and the patient rapidly sank.

CASE 2.—Aged 13, sister of case 1 ; attacked about the same time, and, from what I could learn, in the same manner. I was unfortunate in not seeing this case until the lapse of about four weeks. When I did see the patient, found her in about the same condition as Case 1 at my first visit. After treating the case for some days, the ulcers in the throat gradually healed, but the powers of life were far spent. Like her brother, she had upon her foot a sore caused by the chafing of the shoe. This sore was an ordinary one, showing considerable indisposition to heal, but an ordinary abrasion, till after the throat healed, when to my amazement a regular diphtheritic deposit made its appearance upon the sore, which rapidly passed into an ulcer with the same appearance that was presented in Case 1 ; refusing to granulate, and absolutely maintaining that cold, flatly malignant appearance of the chancre. This ulcer spread by a gradual death of the tissue, not rapid but sure and persistent. In the course of ten or twelve days, gangrene showed itself upon the toes, gradually advancing until the toes were entirely involved. Mortification now made its appearance in the foot around the abrasion caused by the shoe, which spread slowly until it reached a point about three inches above the ankle joint, where a partial line of demarcation was formed, and gradually became more distinct for four days, but finally claimed more, and gangrene slowly continued up the leg until the whole member was involved, and the little patient was relieved from her sufferings.

Very respectfully,

J. W. Lewis.

The two cases reported by Dr. Lewis, where gangrene attacked the extremities several days previous to death, are highly interesting. It appears that these two cases had lingered under the influence of the disease some four weeks previous to the first visit of the Doctor, and that gangrene did not set in till several days after. The diphtheritic exudation on the surface of the abrasion on the foot of each of these patients shows that the morbific cause had pervaded the entire system, and that it is capable of producing a gangrene in the extremities, similar to that which it causes in the original region.

MICROSCOPIC EXAMINATIONS OF EXPECTOR-
ATIONS, EXUDATIONS AND SLOUGHS
IN DIPHTHERIA.

The exudations and sloughs herein examined were taken from the throat and fauces of Amos Bear, December 10th, the sixth day of the disease, and sent to me on the same day by Dr. Effinger. The membranes had the usual appearance of diphtheritic exudations. With them was considerable expectoration or mucous secretion of the anginal region.

The cells of this mucous secretion had a peculiar and interesting appearance. The minute cell contents appeared more distinct than in health, and in many instances were in active and independent motion, moving rapidly among each other and around the large central nuclei. By carefully watching the mucous cells it was also discovered that they too exhibit independent vitality, and had a slow progressive movement mostly in right lines, either singly or in whole columns or in masses. This motion was very slow, but by watching, in many instances, a single cell for hours together, its movements and general metamorphosis were fully and satisfactorily determined. The mucous cells of the spittle and expectoration, as is well known, are the products of the parent epithelial cells, lining the air passages, and those forming the secreting and organizing surfaces of the salivary system. These cells, in a normal or healthy condition, immediately after being formed, have the appearance as seen at a, s and t, Fig. 1, Pl. I.

In the diphtheritic exudations and expectoration, these cells have taken on an increased tendency to be metamorphosed into filaments, each being provided with a minute hair-like appendage and possessing the power of independent motion. These diphtheritic mucous cells are seen at b, c and h, Fig. 1. Pl. I. Their minute cell contents could be readily seen moving independently about among each other and around the central nuclei. As the vitalized mucous cells (b and h) gradually progressed, it was found that the hair-like appendage gradually became larger and longer, till it could be seen to be a tube, into which a portion of the minute cell contents of the mucous cell passed. (c) This metamorphosis or filament development from cells gradually progressed till, after many hours, the cell entirely disappeared, having been spun into a filament like that seen at f. Fig. 1, Pl. I Sometimes from two to many cells would be seen united in a moniliform line, the cells of which would begin to separate, remaining connected by a filament as seen at d, e and m, Fig. 1, Pl. I., and this separation would become greater and greater, until the entire string of cells would be metamorphosed into a long tubular filament containing in it a portion of the minute cell contents of the mucous cells.

The only portions not metamorphosed into filaments were the large central nuclei. This operation of cell metamorphosis was watched day after day for several weeks, till I became fully satisfied that this general active filamentous development of the mucous cells was abnormal, and that from it resulted the membranous exudations of diphtheria. It was satisfactorily determined that the diphtheritic membranes are formed by the rapid metamorphosis of the mucous cells into filaments, which process begins in this disease before they are fairly liberated from the mucous follicles, and even from the parent epithelial tissue.

As the filaments are developed they become interwoven and thus form a more or less thick and compact adherent membrane, according to the activity of the secretion and the cell metamorphosis. The external surfaces of the exuded membranes have the appearance seen at r and q, Fig. 1, Pl. I.

The filaments are so transparent, and their plastic walls become so blended with each other, that it is with difficulty they are distinguished after the membrane is fully formed. In its early stages, however, it can be readily resolved into its ultimate filaments. u. Fig. 1, Pl. I, represents the two kinds of minute cells, highly magnified, that have independent motion in the mucous cells, b. c and i, Fig. 1, Pl. I. p represents the minute cells, highly magnified, seen on the surface of the fragments of exudation q and r. g are masses of sporidia of the sphærotheca pyra—the species that produces blight in the apple, pear and quince trees and decay in their fruit. h, i, k, m, n and o, Fig. 1, Pl. I, represent the mucous cells in the expectoration and exudations of Nancy Bear, in their various stages of metamorphosis. Many other cases have been examined, all of which go to confirm the views here advanced.

SLOUGHS OF ANGINA MALIGNA.

The sloughs from the throat of Amos Bear were subjected to a careful microscopic examination. The bodies represented under Fig. 2, Pl. II, were in the sloughs.

Examinations of like sloughs from Mr. Karn's son and several others, revealed the same bodies with the single exception of the genus anguillila seen at a, Plate VI., Fig. 6, which was only found in the sloughs of Amos Bear, and which probably came from some vinegar gargle he may have used. The minute forms represented at a, Fig. 11, Pl. II are peculiar active bodies, which are really the spores of embryonic filaments of minute species of algæ or fungi. The parent gland cells of animals have the power of taking in and transmitting freely the spores of this vegetation. All organic bodies are filled with these spores, which seem to be quiescent during the physiological states, but as soon as pathological conditions arise they develop and multiply with incredible rapidity. They become very abundant during the fermentation and incipient decay of all organic matter, and especially so in nitrogenized animal tissues. At b, c, d Fig. 2, Pl. II, are represented the mature algoid filaments, which are found in multitudes running in all directions through the exudations and sloughs. e, f, g and h Fig. 2, Pl. II, are cells that have the appearance of being the spores and sporangia of the *mucor malignans* described further on; g and h are more highly magnified than e and f; i appears to be an ascus highly transparent and colorless. k and p. sporidia of the apple blight fungus, (sphærotheca pyra). m. n and o sporidia, single and in mass of the sphærotheca pyra, vegetating with mycelial filaments. These occur abundantly in the sloughs. They are present in large quantities in apple fruit this season and may be carried into the system through the apples eaten. This species of fungus appears to be poisonous to some vegetable tissues, and the sporidia excite irritation of the fauces, trachea and bronchi when inhaled. Another species Spersica (erysiphe graminis) produces the disease known as the *"curl and blister,"* in peach leaves, and which proves so deleterious and destructive to peach orchards. Its known deleterious effects upon vegetation, together with its tendency to irritate the pulmonary membranes when inhaled, renders it probable that it may have some influence in exciting disease in the human subject. At b and x, Fig. 6, Pl. VI, are represented two species of fungous filaments. These are found in the expectoration of diphtheritic patients this season. That represented at x occurs in vast numbers in ripe persimmons this year, in central Ohio. q Fig. 6, Pl. VI. represents a sample of numerous knots of mycelial filaments, that are highly transparent, scattered over the surface of the sloughs, and patches of exudation.

u, v and w Fig. 2, Pl. II, large mucous cells.

Besides the bodies represented under Fig. 2, Pl. II, there were numerous highly transparent large and loosely formed filaments, single and in bundles, that had the appearance of the mycelium, ce.Fig.3, Pl. III, of the mucor malignans. There were, however, no fertile threads. Strongly suspecting that these filaments were fungoid, after cutting off a portion of the slough for further microscopic examination, I placed the balance in a tightly corked two-ounce wide-mouthed bottle, and set it aside in a room where there was no fire. The temperature in this room ranged from 60 to 65° F. In a few days after being set aside, a white mould or fertile thread began to appear on the surface of the slough. This mould gradually increased till on December 28th, it enveloped the entire surface with a mass of white fertile threads that resembled fine cotton. On examining this under the microscope, I found the surface fertile threads to emanate from the same mycelium as was noticed running all through the slough and exudation on Dec. 10th, when freshly separated.

At that time, however, there were no signs of fertile threads, and the mycelium was very much more transparent and less firm than on Dec. 28th. On placing this mycelium and fertile threads under the microscope, a most beautiful fungus in full fruit was exhibited, samples of which are seen at a, b, c, d, e and u, Fig. 3; Pl. III. d represents the threads of the mycelium packed together and filled with minute cells and granules, and covered often as at e

with minute cells. Mingled with the threads were numerous highly transparent spore-like bodies, that had no connection with them. This fungus appears to belong to the *genus mucor*. Not having met anywhere with a description of this species, I have named it the *malignans*, as at this stage of the investigation it seems to have something to do as the cause of malignant diphtheria, as will more fully appear further on.

a represents a fertile filament bearing three grape-like clusters of sporangia. These bodies resemble mucous cells, and appear like the cells of diphtheritic exudation and expectoration. The mycelium and minute cells are matted together in the exudation and sloughs of diphtheria, and covered with clusters of large cells, somewhat as seen at u, Fig. 3, Pl. III. Often however, the large cells are mostly absent.

b, Fig. 3, Pl. III, represents a fertile filament, covered with fruit or sporangias in an early stage of developement. m represents the minute cells highly magnified, that fill the large cells.

g, n, s and t Fig.3 Pl. III, represent numerous active bodies moving about among the filaments, and which are seen at a,Fig.2,Pl.II.

v,Fig.3,Pl. III, represents the mature fruit after it has separated from the fertile threads. These cells are what I have found frequently in diphtheritic exudation. They so much resemble mucous cells that they would readily be mistaken for them. I had supposed them to be mucous cells until I obtained the mature plants producing fruit.

The minute bodies at w, Fig. 3, Pl. III, are what appear to be the spores of the mucor malignans.

Diphtheria Produced by Inhaling the Spores of the Mucor Malignans.—On the 28th of December, before opening the bottle containing the diphtheritic slough and exudation, covered with white mould, I locked myself in my room and opened the windows to prevent exposing the rest of the family to the disease. All the food I took for the next three days was hastily passed to me by my wife through the door slightly opened.

I was determined to make careful microscopic examinations and drawings of the fungus, with full description of all the circumstances and conditions, no matter what might be the result to me.

In removing the cork from the bottle, the slight jar sent the light spores out of the mouth of the bottle, appearing like the spores flying from a compressed "puff ball." These I freely inhaled.

In a few minutes I had the vegetation under the microscope, and was making my drawings of the plant which are represented in Plate III., Fig. 3.

My throat and fauces began to get dry, hot and feverish almost immediately after inhaling the spores. In less than thirty minutes, the same symptoms excited in the throat and fauces had extended down the trachea and bronchi, and seemingly into the air cells. With the dry, congested, hot feeling, was a heavy, persistent, dull pain, as if the parts affected were partially hepatized and useless. There was a feeling of oppression about the whole chest, and the breathing unsatisfactory and labored. These feelings became more and more intensified, so that in a few hours I was almost incapacitated from going on with the microscopic work and drawings. The spores had passed so freely and deeply into the air passages, and the oppression and irritation of the parts was so intensified, that I began to fear that I should not be able to pursue the investigation further, unless I could get relief.

Believing the cause of my suffering to be the spores inhaled, I immediately began taking one grain of quinia sulph. every thirty minutes; and also to inhale and snuff an equal amount at the same time. In addition to this, I gargled a strong solution of tinc. ferri chloridi every time my throat became dry and sticky. In a short time the troublesome irritation in the throat, fauces and air passages began to be relieved, so that I was comparatively comfortable and able to go on with the microscopic work and drawings.

I am fully satisfied from what occurred during the attack and from my subsequent experience with the disease, that I should probably not have recovered if I had not treated myself heroically, as I did; for the mucous membranes of the entire air passages were inoculated with the cause of the most malignant type of diphtheria I have ever met with.

The quinine, taken internally and inhaled every half hour, kept the system and surfaces so saturated with it that the vegetation could make but little headway, and consequently the disease was comparatively light and soon overcome. The disease was accompanied by a ropy, adhesive exudation, which excited hawking and spitting frequently. The same state extended down the œsophagus, and into the stomach and intestines.

Bowels (which were before regular and in fine, healthy condition) became constipated, and fæces hard and plastic. During the night there was considerable burning, heavy pain in the stomach and bowels, aggravated by lying on the abdomen, and eased by lying on the back. There was scarcely any tenderness on pressure. Counter irritation produced no relief.

On the following morning, the first mucus that was coughed up contained many of the bodies v and the spores w, Fig. 3, Plate III. Hawking to dislodge the adhesive mucus would excite hiccoughing, while but little matter would be raised. Coughing aggravated the pain.

Dec. 30th and 31st.—All the symptoms were aggravated. On the 30th there was considerable fever, with a dry, hot, heavy, congested feeling of the whole mucous lining of the air passages and œsophagus, stomach and intestines. Urine became scanty and high-colored, and deposited a large sediment. There was a dry, pricking, constricting feeling in the throat and fauces, with a sticking together of the part. The mucous secretions from the air passages and mouth were ropy and filamentous, and the mucous cells had the appearance seen at Fig. 1, Plate I.

There was also pain in the sides of the neck, in the thyroid cartilage, and in the parotid and sub-maxillary glands. During the night, slept well.

Dec. 31st. The back part of the throat and fauces were covered with diphtheritic exudations. The mucous membrane of the air passages and digestive canal felt less congested and hot, and the secretions of the bronchi and fauces were less ropy, and had less tendency to pass into filamentous metamorphosis. Bowels less constipated. Urine still scanty and high colored, with a large sediment.

1863. January 1st.—Still better. The exudation patches in the throat are disappearing, and the secretions of the air passages less ropy, and bowels quite regular, appetite good. Continue the quinine sulph. every half hour.

January 4th.—Have been constantly improving since the first. The diphtheritic patches have entirely disappeared, and feel quite well except a heavy, aching pain in the laryngeal and pharyngeal region, with a slight difficulty in perfect articulation.

This latter result is of frequent occurrence after recovery from severe attacks. Often this partial paralysis of the anginal region lasts for some days after recovery from the disease.

A good illustration of the contagiousness of the disease occurred in this instance. Notwithstanding the precautions taken, about eight days after the appearance of the first symptoms in my case, my wife was taken down with the disease. The only exposure she had was in passing the food to me through the slightly opened door, and this only for a moment, three times a day. Her attack was sudden and severe, and required energetic treatment to prevent the exudation from extending into the bronchi. Two days after her attack, her sister was taken down, and on the following day her brother. All recovered.

Blood in Diphtheria.—The blood corpuscles of malignant diphtheria are plastic and sticky, and have a peculiar tendency to adhere together, and to filamentous metamorphosis, showing that the disease is not local but systemic, probably influencing and modifying the organizing functions of the parent cells of the lacteal and lymphatic systems and spleen—in short, the entire parent gland cell tissue.

At Fig. 4, Plate IV., are seen the various abnormal conditions and bodies of the blood of angina maligna. At a and b are seen masses of cells, resembling diphtheritic anginal cells. They are, however, colorless corpuscles formed by the spleen and the lacteal and lymphatic glands, and contain the micrococcus spores of the diphtheritic fungus.

This peculiar tendency to stick together and become aggregated in irregular masses is abnormal.

At c c, Fig. 4, Pl. IV, are thin, pliable sacks, constantly changing in shape, filled with minute, vitalized granules constantly in motion—protoplasmic.

The sacks have an amœba-like motion, and communicate with the cavities of the cells b, and their contents are the minute cell contents of these cells. d represents these minute, independently moving granules, more highly magnified. e a cell like those at i and b, Fig. 1, Pl. I, having a hair-like appendage, it having taken on and commenced the process of filamentous metamorphosis. f rhomboid epithelial cells, that are removed from their attachment and are floating in the blood. g a large cell passing into a filament. At h and k are represented algoid filaments that occur in little groups and skeins in the blood.

Attached to the filaments k are many spores of the vegetation. m and n are masses of fibrin, through and in which are seen algoid filaments. i filaments resembling filamentous neurine. This kind of filament was frequently met with in the blood of Amos Bear. All these bodies occur abundantly in the blood, showing a formulative condition, and a disposition in its cells to become metamorphosed into filaments, and a tendency in these filaments to become aggregated in masses, forming clots. This explains why there is a disposition to gangrene—from a kind of embolism in this malignant form of the disease, the algoid spores and filaments and spores, and the blood aggregating, forming masses, clots and emboli choking up the capillary vessels, so as to impede and in some cases entirely stop the circulation.

Urine in Diphtheria.—The lining membrane of the urinary organs also takes on diphtheritic functional derangements. In all cases of diphtheria, there is the same peculiar, flocculent, pinkish-white deposit, made up of minute granules of urates, like those at Fig. 5, Pl. IV. With these are many crystals of lithic acid, often very large, and having the appearance of those seen at a, b, c, d and f, Fig. 5, Plate IV.

With these are frequently found cystine and the peculiar crystalline forms seen at e, d, and k, Fig. 5, Plate IV.

Also epithelial cells and their products, undergoing the filamentous metamorphosis, with many algoid filaments.

At i are represented crystals of the lithates of soda and ammonia, which frequently occur in diphtheritic urine. w and v¹, Fig. 7, Plate VI, represent peculiar mucous cells, ruptured by their minute cell contents escaping. q and q¹, Fig. 6, Pl. V, spherical algoid cells uniting into moniliform filaments. g fungoid filaments. h and l the so called vibriones, which are united into embryonic algoid or fungoid filaments. m and m¹, Fig. 6, Plate V, algoid or fungoid filaments already formed, in which no structure can be made out. t, u, v and w, Fig. 6, Plate V, various stages in the formation of algoid filaments, from the so-called vibrio. r and s are highly magnified.

The bodies here represented in diphtheritic urine, under Fig. 5, Pl. IV, are the result of careful microscopic examinations of the urine of twenty-three cases of well marked diphtheria. In one case that has come under my observation, through Dr. Effinger, the attending physician, the diphtheritic derangements were wholly confined to the bladder, it never producing any abnormal anginal conditions that were noticed by the patient. The patient was a married lady, this attack occurring while she was attending on her husband, who lay sick with ordinary diphtheria (angina membranacea).

Treatment.—During the twenty years that have elapsed since making these investigations and preparing this paper, I have treated several hundred cases of diphtheria with quinine sulphate and tinct. ferri chloridi, and I can only call to mind the loss of a single case, and that was a German boy, who would not take the medicine with any regularity. The quinia sulphate should be given by the mouth, in powder, every half hour, keeping the mouth, fauces and throat constantly covered and saturated with it— also snuff and inhale it at the same time, so as to keep the surfaces of the entire air passages covered and saturated with it.

In addition to this I have used the following as a gargle:—

R. Tinct. ferri chloridi........ ℨ j
   Aqua .... ℥ viij
S. Gargle every hour.

R. Carbolic acid (cryst. white).. ℨ j
   Salicylic Acid............ ℨ ss
   Water.................. ℥ xii
   Pure glycerine.... .... ℥ iv
   Ol. menth. pip............gtt. xv
S. Gargle every half hour before taking the quinia sulphate.

The quinia sulphate is the remedy to be depended upon for checking the development of the case.

There are many little things to be done to relieve and make more comfortable, such as hop poultices around the neck, so covered in as to bring the steam from the hops up around the mouth, where it is inhaled. This often soothes and relieves the suffocating and croupy condition in children. The swallowing of small bits of ice often aids in loosening up the particles of exudation.

Penciling the throat with alcohol also relieves the sufferings of the patient.

If quinine cannot be obtained, any antiseptic remedy, or any medicine that will check or control the fermentation in a yeast-pot, or preserve meat from spoiling, will be useful in aiding the cure. Among these may be mentioned permanganate of potash, sulphites, all the mineral acids, salt, borax, benzoate of soda, potassium chlorate, salicylic acid, carbolic acid, tinct. ferri chloridi, bromine, iodine, sulphur, &c , &c.

In certain conditions where the cough is croupy, and the membranes tough, and expectoration adhesive and ropy, with a strong tendency for the disease to invade the trachea and bronchi, small doses of mercurial, often administered, check or control this dangerous tendency, so that the exudations become softer, membranes less adhesive, croupy cough ceases, and the patient begins to improve.

Scarlatina, the Symptoms and Derangements of; Similar to those of Diphtheria.— The mucous cells of the anginal exudation of scarlatina, with the bodies found in the blood and urine, present marked similarities to those of diphtheria.

In both diseases there is a strong tendency for the cell products of parent epithelial cells to undergo filamentous metamorphosis.

The disease in both cases appears to emanate from functional derangements in the organizing processes of the ultimate epithelial cells, and in part appears to result in a too rapid development of cells into filaments. The primary cause of both diseases, however, must consist in some morbific agent, which operates upon these cells, poisoning the nutrient products which they originate, so that after a certain limited period, which is the period of incubation, the whole system begins to sympathize, and take on a series of abnormal actions, which are simply systemic efforts to eliminate from the organism the morbific poison, and which actions constitute the symptoms or peculiarities of the disease. In this light the functional derangements in the organic processes of epithelial cells, become simply a resultant action excited by the primary cause of the disease, and is one of the efforts of nature to eradicate morbific matter, by accelerating normal changes in organic processes.

It should therefore be the constant care of the physician, not to run counter to nature in her efforts to cure the disease, but simply to so equalize, aid and modify her actions, as to alleviate suffering and guard against dangerous results.

With these few preliminary remarks we proceed to the microscopic examination of the expectoration, exudation, blood, urine and the desquamated cuticle of scarlatina.

Expectoration and Exudation.—The peculiar abnormal and similar tendency to the filamentous development of the mucous cells of the expectorated and exuded products of scarlatina and diphtheria, renders it evident that the anginal epithelial functional derangements in both diseases are remarkably similar. This similarity is found also to extend to the abnormal products of the blood and urine. This makes it conclusive that the same systemic, epithelial, functional derangements are common to both diseases. The results here obtained are confirmatory of Dr. Tweedie's supposition previously given.

Fig. 7, Plate VI, represents the appearance of the mucous cells of the expectoration and exudation of scarlatina angina. By comparing the filamentous metamorphosis going on in these cells with that exhibited at Fig. 1, Pl. I, a remarkable similarity will be noticed.

a. Fig. 7, Pl. VI, represents the normal mucous cell immediately after being formed and before it takes on the active condition, or begins to manifest independent activity. b, c and h are mucous cells in scarlatina, in the active stage. The most of the cells in this stage have a single fine caudal filament, resembling an extremely fine hair, tapering from the cell, and projecting from its posterior side, or from the side opposite to the direction in which it moves. Sometimes there are two or even three hair-like processes visible. The length of these hair like processes in the early stages is usually from two to three times the diameter of the cell.

The motion of these cells is a very slow, uniform, progressive one, often so slow that even an experienced eye would fail to detect it, unless the attention was called particularly to it, and the observations continued on the same cell often for hours. By selecting,however, a single cell standing alone, and keeping the eye on it for some time, a perceptible movement is plainly manifest.

In this stage of development or metamorphosis, the cells are usually more or less elongated, though they often appear spherical. They have the power of changing their shape, sometimes appearing very much elongated,at other times slightly oval, and then spherical.

All of these forms are noticed frequently within a brief space of time, in the same cell, while watching its motions.

The elongation is always in the direction in which the cell moves. Before the cell becomes active the hair-like appendage (cilium) cannot be seen, and in many instances after motion has commenced these processes are so fine that it is impossible to detect them,even by the best glasses. These cells contain a large central single or compound nucleus, around which are numerous minute spherical and oval granules or cells, many of which are in active motion.

Those in active motion are probably sperm cells to these organisms, and the others germ cells.

Following the stage of independent activity comes that of filamentous metamorphosis. During this period the activity is slight,being confined to very slow, almost imperceptible,forward motion,which takes place at short intervals, or appears to be somewhat periodic. The hair-like projection becomes elongated and enlarged in calibre, and soon is seen to be a membranous tube. As this tube enlarges and elongates, the contents of the mucous cells (consisting of fluid and minute granules) pass into it, and the minute cells usually become arranged in a single moniliform row along its cavity, as seen at z Fig. 1,Plate I, d, e, l, m and i,Fig. 7, Plate VI. As the contents of the mucous

cell pass into the tubular filament, it (the cell) grows smaller, and smaller till finally it entirely disappears, leaving simply the resultant filament.*

Often two or more cells are united by one or more tubular filaments, i, m, Fig. 7, Pl. VI, z, Fig. 1, Pl. I.

Sometimes two or more filaments proceed from the same cell, as seen at l, Fig. 7, Pl. VI. The number of filaments is determined by the number of hair-like processes, and these are increased as the tendency to filamentous metamorphosis is increased beyond the normal standard. At m two mucous cells have entirely emptied their minute cell contents into the connecting filaments. After the cells have disappeared, we have simple filaments, as seen at p and q, Fig. 7, Plate VI. Often the mucous cells arrange themselves in moniliform rows, as at n and o, Fig. 7, Plate VI.

r are the minute cells and moniliform short filaments that make up the contents of the mucous cells. These are highly magnified. At the extremity of the forming filaments at g, Fig. 7, Plate VI, short, active, moniliform lines of minute cells and single cells are escaping. This has only been noticed in a few instances.

u spores of the saccharomycetes cerevisiæ, which occur through the mucus singly and in short, branching, moniliform rows.

s and t highly refractive, oblate spheroidal cells of a pearly appearance, containing bodies resembling spores. t is an edge view and s a side view. In the right hand

---

* Here is described briefly an interesting organic process, one from which, when physiologically, or slowly and healthfully performed,emanate all the filaments of the muscular, fibrous and nerve tissues of the animal body,but which, when the metamorphosis is too hasty or rapid, becomes an abnormal action, resulting in a preponderance of solids, and, in consequence, congestions and exudations, the damming up of the capillary blood streams, checking and even stopping circulation locally, which may produce the pathological states of inflammation and gangrene. This subject will be more fully treated in another paper.

cell at s are short filaments with the spores. The spores are of a reddish transparent orange color.

Many of these cells are entirely empty. When mature they fracture from the circumference towards the center at numerous points, allowing the spore contents to escape. They are quite numerous in the exudations, and are the same as b and c, Fig. 8, Plate VII, in the urine.

The expectoration and exudation in scarlatina contain numerous confervoid filaments, like those at h, f, Fig. 6, Plate V. e, n, i, Fig. 8, Plate VII., of the urine of the same disease.

Blood of Scarlatina.—The appearance of the abnormal bodies in the blood of scarlatina anginosa is so nearly identical with those seen under diphtheria, Fig. 4, Plate IV., that they will not require repetition here.

Desquamated Cuticle of Scarlatina.— Dec. 19th. Placed about four grains of desquamated cuticle from a scarlatina patient in a watch glass, with a little pure water, tightly covered and set aside at a temperature of 65° Fahr. The dry cuticle was made up of flat, scale-like epithelial cells, each containing a large central nucleus, surrounded by minute cells or granules.

Twenty-four hours after the large central nuclei, s and s¹, Fig. 9, Plate VII, of the epithelial cells n and q had taken an independent motion, and were moving about in the epithelial cells and escaping.

After having escaped from the epithelial cells, the minute, hair-like appendages could be quite distinctly seen, as at a and b, Fig. 9, Plate VII.

The movements were very much more active than I had previously noticed in the epithelial cell products of mucous surfaces. c represents the cells a and b after the hairlike processes have begun to enlarge into a tubular filament.

d represents the spores of a minute algoid vegetation, that have escaped from the flattened epithelial cells. These spores move independently in all directions.

c, f and k represent these spores united into moniliform filaments.

m represents a blunt, tubular filament (algoid) with cells united in twos.

g and h represent short, algoid filaments with cells united in twos and threes, and the lines of demarcation between the individual cells obliterated.

r represents a long, algoid or fungoid filament, with no appearance of cross lines or cells. The inside cells have united into a uniform inside tube.

All of these filaments have the power of independent motion.

The motions are slow, and consist of the waving or vibrating of their extremities— leptothrix? l is a diatom from the water drank. u probably the urate of soda. x crystal, probably phosphate of lime.

Urine of Scarlet Fever.—Fig. 8, Plate VII, represents the various abnormal bodies found in the urine of scarlatina, when the disease is at its height. a, b and e represent a peculiar kind of flattened, oblate spheroidal cells, containing orange-colored sporoid bodies. a and b represent side views, and an edge view. They belong to the same class of bodies as s and t, v and w, Fig. 7, Plate VI. They occur frequently in the urine.

d represents cells from the parent epithelial cells of the bladder. They are single, and also aggregated in masses, and many of them manifest a disposition to filamentous metamorphosis. e, Fig. 8, Plate V., and f and g, Fig. 6, Plate V., algoid filaments, made up of an outside tube enclosing a moniliform line of minute spheroidal or oval cells, bearing a close resemblance to anabaina mollis.

h r, Fig. 6, Plate V., represent a species of leptothrix. Attached to the filament h are a number of short ones, belonging to the genus anabaina. These short moniliform filaments are the prevailing ones in scarlatina urine, a single drop often containing many hundred. i, k and l, Fig. 8, Plate VII., a species of hypheothrix which is quite frequently met with. o large rhomboid crystals of lithic acid. These are quite abundant.

w, Fig. 1, Plate I., a large, partially collapsed, membranous sack, resembling those found in the tomato or apple, and is probably accidentally present. Fig. 8, Plate VII., r r r crystals of creatine. The crystalline forms s, t and u are also sometimes met with.

Some General Remarks connected with the Pathology of Fevers, and the Tissues upon which Fever Poisons Primarily Act.—The first layer of cell organisms, through which food, medicinal agents and poisons have to pass in entering the animal body, is the epithelial.

It is very evident that medicinal agents and poisons must act upon these cells, modifying their organizing and nutritive functions, and the derangement produced must first exist in these cells, and secondarily the more highly animalized elements and tissues beyond become affected, through the poisoned and medicated products furnished them by the epithelial tissue.

There is hence evidence for believing that all febrile diseases, eruptive and otherwise, are intimately connected with functional and structural derangements of the cells of epithelial tissue. So intimate is the relation that these functional and structural derangements appear to constitute the disease. The different functional and structural disturbances of the various portions of the epithelial structure would seem to give rise to the various types of fevers. The primary causes of these functional and structural derangements in most fevers are varied, numerous and obscure, while in others which are contagious they are more defined, each being excited only by a particular, specific cause.

Before entering upon a few general remarks on the ætiology, &c., of fevers, indicated by microscopic investigations of the epithelial system in pyrexial states, I will briefly refer to some generally received views on these diseases.

In primary fevers there is a general pyrexial state, without any evident patholog-ical lesion, there being, to the unaided eye, no observable localized disease.

As all organs and tissues appear to participate in the febrile action, when it is once established, its seat appears, and is supposed to be, no more in one tissue than in another. It has however been noticed that the first symptoms of the manifest invasion present themselves through the nervous system.

It has therefore been supposed probable that the "fever poison" first invades the animal system through the channel of the nerves. These nerve symptoms, however, will be shown further on to be probably but secondary results in the invasion.

Cullen's definition of fever, modified by Christison, is as follows : "After a preliminary stage of languor, weakness and defective appetite, acceleration of the pulse, increased heat, great debility of the limbs and disturbance of most of the functions without primary local disease."

The great French anatomic schools, composed of able investigators, advanced a theory, which was generally entertained throughout Europe.

This theory regarded fever as the "constitutional result, and its symptoms as the general expression throughout the system, of the effects of a localized process of disease, having for its constant seat a part of the intestinal canal.

In fevers there is an increase of temperature above the natural standard of about 4° Fahr. ; even during the algid stage of the disease, the elevation of temperature is present.

This has been noticed to be a constant morbid condition of fevers. It is now generally admitted that the chief source of the increased temperature in fevers, arises from increased activity of the causes which operate in the production of the healthy temperature.

The source of healthy animal heat is held to be developed by the nutrient changes perpetually going on in the tissues.

An able enquirer—Virchow—assumes that the nutrient metamorphosis of the tissues is increased in fever, and as a natural and necessary consequence, this gives rise to increase of temperature. This nutrient metamorphosis consists of those organizing changes going on both in nutrient materials supplied to the system, and those interstitial changes by which the constituents of the body themselves are metamorphosed and removed. Virchow supposed that this increased metamorphosis was the consequence of some internal, excitant cause, the real nature of which is unknown.

Lyon, in his work on fevers, p. 33, says : " Some facts determined by recent investigations and experiments would appear to show that the first steps in the establishment of febrile conditions are not to be sought for in the blood itself, or in any part of the circulating apparatus, but to indicate certain deranged conditions of the nervous system as more likely to furnish us with an explanation at once natural and proper on this point." Virchow believed that the elevation of animal temperature in fevers arose from a kind of paralytic condition of the nervous system. This is supposed to have been well established by numerous experiments. Becquerel, Brescher and Helmboltz, in experiments on that kind of nervous irritation which excites muscular contraction, found that it increased animal temperature. In opposition to this, Bernard has proved that section of the sympathetic nerve in the neck is followed by rapid increase of temperature in the corresponding half of the head. Brown Séquard's experiments are to the same effect. Weber has shown that the heart's action is arrested by the irritation of the vagi nerves. It has long been known that section of these nerves causes acceleration of the pulse.

Ludwig and Hoffa have shown that in moderate irritation of the vagi, the lateral pressure of blood in the arteries is lessened ; while Volkman and Towelin have determined that it increased after section of the nerves. Fraube has found that digitalis acts as an irritating stimulant upon the regulating nerves of the heart, and that a diminished temperature is produced by it, which he attributes to the diminished velocity of the blood stream.

From these experiments it has been inferred by authors " that the causes that regulate the velocity, tension and other physical conditions of the blood stream and the vessels which carry it, seem unquestionably to reside in the nervous system, which exercises a sort of regulator or moderator function over the circulation, and through the circulation over the animal temperature."

Cullen held that " the first link in the chain of fever actions, was a depressed brain and nervous system." The spasm (or tonic contraction) of the capillaries, he considered as resulting from the depression of the brain and nervous centers, and that the reaction of the circulation was an effort to overcome this state of spasm of the extreme vessels. After the tissues have become once deranged by being nourished with abnormal food, organized by epithelial cells deranged in their functions, we might well expect to find them in a diseased, irritated condition, which would manifest itself by a train of abnormal symptoms, which would continue until the exciting cause was removed.

With regard to the elevation of animal heat, we would state in this connection some few facts which go to show that animal heat may to a considerable extent be developed by the organizing processes of epithelial cells. After animal life has ceased, we have known the temperature of the body of a horse twelve hours after death (temperature of atmosphere 40°Fah.) to stand at 160° Fah. This high temperature arose mostly from the rapid organic changes going on in epithelial tissue, and from interstitial tissue dissolution. We have known the body of a dog, poisoned with veratrine, twelve hours after death to stand at 90° Fah. In the development of yeast cells in fermentation, the temperature of the fermenting mass often rises (where large masses of matter are fermenting), to from 120° to 150° Fah.

In the decay of nitrogenized tissues the

temperature sometimes rises even above
150° Fah.

In the rapid interstitial changes going on
in fevers, we might well expect to find an
elevated temperature of the animal
body.

After the phenomena noticed in the microscopic examinations of the epithelial cells
in various parts of the epithelial structure,
in health, during the period of febrile incubation, and after the manifest invasion of
the disease, there appears to be evidence
for believing that the nervous system is not
the department of the organism first en-
croached upon, or the avenue through
which the exciting cause of fever first pass-
es, in invading the animal system.

There is a cell structure making up a
considerable portion of the organism, which
possesses a life independent of the animal
body, the cells of which vegetate and develop after animal vitality ceases, as has
been fully shown in the preceding pages.

This tissue is composed of cells, the function of which is to assimilate and organize
the nutrient matters of the food into the various products which are designed to be appropriated in building up and nourishing the
various tissues of the animal body. It is
known by the name of epithelial tissue, and
makes up the organizing portion of all
glandular masses and surfaces. The cells
of this tissue are extra-vascular, and so far
as known, not supplied with nerves. All
the external surfaces of, and avenues of approach to, the more highly animalized parts
of the system are covered and guarded in
all and every part by these epithelial cells.
Nothing can enter the system without first
passing through the cells of this assimilat-
ing and organizing epithelial envelope. This
epithelial envelope is the ultimate basis of
the entire organic structure. Its individual cells are the avenues and apparatus
through which all the nutrient materials of
the food have to pass, and be assimilated and organized, ere they are fitted to
nourish and sustain the various tissues.

The tissues themselves, outside of epithelial or glandular cells, have no power within

themselves of organizing matter from food
for their support. The epithelial cells are
the avenues through which alimentary, medicinal and morbific agents reach the systemic tissues, and are the ultimate bases of
many important physiological and pathological processes.

All febrile excitants must consequently
act primarily upon the cells of this tissue,
deranging their organizing functions so as to
impart abnormal properties to the matters
organized.

The period from the commencement of
the action of the deranging influences upon
these cells to the time when the abnormal
organized products begin to produce perceptible derangements in the nerve and
other tissues which these organized matters
nourish, is the period of incubation. Of
the different types of morbific agents which
produce the different types of disease, each
acts in its own peculiar way upon these cells
of extravascular life, producing in them
specific changes in their organizing functions, which in each case results in a particular type of disease.

This matter will be more fully set forth
in a paper in progress on the "Ultimate
structure and functions of epithelial (glandular) tissue, and how influenced in function
by morbific agents."

It is through the cells of this tissue that
most of our medicinal agents and poisons produce their beneficial or baneful results.

The study of the specific action of the
various agents of the materia medica, &c.,
upon the gland cells, opens up a new and
rich field for careful investigation, which
will yet result in the discovery of ultimate
organic actions and cardinal truths that will
tend to reduce the healing art more to an
exact science, and establish unvarying
guides in many instances for the practition-
er. It is in studying the functions of this
primordial structure in health and disease,
and under the influence of medicinal agents,
that we may expect to find much that is
new and true respecting those obscure ultimate physiological and pathological changes

and medicinal effects which lie at the very foundation of medical science, and which are so important to understand in order to free the practice of medicine from an empiricism which has ever clung to it in defiance of past research.

In fevers the organizing cells (epithelial) become dry, parched, and are so poisoned by morbific agents that their normal functions of organizing cells are much deranged, and to a great extent cease.

Nutrient materials introduced into the stomach not being, save to a limited extent, assimilated and organized, act as foreign bodies, producing irritation of the intestinal canal and system generally. On the other hand interstitial death and decay become rapid, producing debility, emaciation, &c. This state of things necessarily results in the long train of symptoms attendant upon fevers.

The rapid interstitial changes are efforts on the part of nature to purge the system of morbific materials which have already been organized and become incorporated in the tissues during the period of incubation. This morbific matter must be disposed of or eliminated before recovery can take place.

The symptoms in any given case of fever are but the expressions of the extent to which the morbific poisoning has invaded the tissues, and of the efforts on the part of nature to rid the system of the poisoned epithelial products already appropriated, and the tendency to check the further organization of products for nutrient purposes, until the system becomes purged of the fever poison. This explains the reason why it is so useless to attempt to "break up" well established fevers, except by removing or rendering inert the morbific cause. In pure fevers there are no perceptible organic lesions. The disease is one of function instead of structure. The primary seat of the derangement is in the ultimate epithelial cells, the very basement structure of the organism. In *eruptive fevers* the cutaneous surface becomes involved, and there is also a tendency for the mucous and serous sur-

faces to take on like pathological conditions. These fevers are distinguished from each other by the character of the surface lesions. In scarlatina and measles there is a peculiar tendency for the mucous membranes to become involved. The former is commonly attended with a peculiar and characteristic form of sore throat (diphtheritic),while the latter is usually accompanied by a watery exudation from the eyes and nose (coryza, and a bronchial affection varying in extent and importance.

In *small-pox* there is a tendency to lesion of the serous surfaces (the pleura especially) and occasionally the mucous coats of the intestines are involved (pustules on the mucous intestinal surfaces).

In eruptive fevers and typhus, one attack gives a peculiar protective immunity against its recurrence in the same individual. The cause of this protective immunity may possibly be arrived at by carefully studying the changes impressed upon the ultimate epithelial cells by the specific causes of these diseases.*

The spores of many algæ and fungi and perhaps other cryptogams produce a febrile condition of the mucous lining of the air passages when inhaled. This febrile condition is local, and confined to the delicate parent epithelial cell surfaces with which the spores come in immediate contact. It often lasts from one to several hours after removal from exposure to the morbific cause. In walking over, disturbing, or pitching old, mouldy straw or hay, the throat, mouth and fauces become dry, hot and parched, and there is a constant desire to swallow, hawk and spit, with an almost entire suppression of the normal secretions of these surfaces. Very soon this dry, congested sensation extends into and throughout the air passages of the lungs, and is there accompanied by a heavy, congested feeling.

---

* The length of time that this impress of immunity lasts in any given case is determined by the length of the life and existence of the epithelial cells receiving the impress. Our epithelial cell envelope is constantly dying, disintegrating and disappearing and new cells are formed to take their place, so that the integrity of the envelope is constantly preserved.

In walking over "peaty ague bogs," where the surface is broken, exposing the fresh soil covered with ague vegetation, during the months of July, August and September, or in passing through the heavy night air and vapors in malarial districts, the same or similar febrile sensations to those from mouldy straw and hay are experienced.[*]

These sensations often last for hours, and sometimes during an entire day, after removal from the morbific cause. On examining the expectorated mucus, it is found filled with fungoid and algoid spores, and fragments of fungoid filaments. We have them here *an exciting cause of local febrile excitement,* which any one may be fully satisfied of by exposing himself to the condition just described. That the morbific poison in these cases is cryptogamic, there is no possible doubt, as in hundreds of instances in our observations, where this febrile condition of the air passages has been excited, the expectorated mucus has been found to contain uniformly fungoid and algoid bodies in great numbers: and further, these bodies were the only foreign substances in the mucus that was constantly present in such cases.

The atmosphere in certain localities, especially the heavy, damp, night atmosphere, is often found loaded, during the season of active cryptogamic development, with the invisible spores of numerous microscopic cryptogams, that multiply and develop with great prolificness, some upon living, some upon diseased, and others upon dead and decaying organic tissues.

This established, we may go one step further and reasonably conclude *that bodies which are capable of exciting local fever in the epithelial surfaces with which they come in contact, by a few minutes exposure to them, may, by frequent and long exposure of the system to the same cause, become so diffused*

---

[*] That this local febrile excitement acts primarily upon the epithelial cells is evident from the fact that the first abnormal indication noticed is the suppression of the epithelial cell secretion; the throat, fauces, bronchi and pulmonary membranes becoming dry, parched, &c.

throughout the organism by being inhaled and taken into it with the food and drink, as to communicate their morbific properties to the entire epithelial surfaces of the intestinal canal, and the lacteal, lymphatic, glandular and vascular epithelial surfaces, and so derange the functions of the organizing cells as to render the products organized by them, for the nourishment of the nervous and all other tissues of the body, poisonous. As soon as these poisoned nutrient products become appropriated by the tissues, to a certain extent, the system gives way to those powerful efforts of nature, which are designed, not only to prevent as far as possible the further introduction of the fever poison, but by rapid interstitial changes eliminate from the organism the poisoned organized matters that have already been appropriated by the tissues during the period of incubation.

The sum of these manifestations of nature constitutes the disease known as fever.

These remarks apply to all fevers, and especially to those which are not regarded as contagious. In those that are contagious there are generally surface lesions in the shape of eruptions. In this class, called eruptive, the morbific cause is no doubt of a similar character to that of other fevers, but seems to possess in addition the peculiar property of those organisms known as "yeast plants," capable of multiplying almost infinitely in the animal system from a small beginning. The animal system to this vegetation seems to be a prolific "hot bed," in which they develop and multiply and extend without limit. *They also possess the peculiar property of impressing upon the epithelial cell system the power of resisting to a remarkable extent subsequent invasions of the same disease.*

It has been, however, observed, that as the period lengthens from the time of the first invasion of the disease to subsequent exposures, the tendency becomes greater and greater, or the epithelial cell system has less and less power to resist a second invasion.

This is an interesting field for inquiry. I will here suggest what appears to point in this direction, and which may be found on careful and extended research to be the true cause of this susceptibility to a second invasion.

The parent epithelial cells are to a considerable degree permanent and independent organisms. Each has its attachment, and carries on its own organic processes, more or less independent of its neighbor. These parent cells are the bodies through which fever poisons gain access to the system. They are the bodies that are deranged in their organizing functions by fever poisons, and the organisms that must receive the more or less permanent prophylactic or resisting impress. This impress, upon any given epithelial cell, is no doubt permanent. It has been observed, and I have no doubt of its truth, that these parent epithelial organisms from time to time, and from a variety of causes, die, disintegrate and disappear, while new parent cells develop to take their place.

In process of time, varying greatly in different persons, a great share of the original epithelial cell structures that had at some previous period received from an invasion of one of this class of diseases a protective impress, may have passed away, and a new system of epithelial cells taken their place. This new system of epithelial cells, having never been invaded, are, of course, like the first, susceptible of invasion, and in such case there would be a second attack of the disease in the same individual. This attack would vary in intensity with the proportion of new epithelial cells in the glandular surface (each epithelial cell may be regarded to all intents and purposes a glana). If there are but few, the tendency to the second attack would be very slight—so slight that it would not be attended with any eruption, and with but slight febrile symptoms.

This is what every physician has often noticed in his own case, when attending upon contagious fevers.

I trust the investigations and few remarks here offered will interest the serious consideration of medical observers in this interesting field of inquiry.

I am satisfied that careful observation of the epithelial cell organisms, the study in detail of their ultimate and all-important functions, will not only be highly interesting to the observer, but will inspire him with that confidence he has seldom before felt, that his researches are now in the way of ultimate and important physiological and pathological truths, the solution of which has resisted past research, and which are destined to remove many remnants of empiricism from the healing art, and reduce it more to a science of unvarying principles.

It is only by the study in detail of this organizing cell system that we may expect to discover those primary and ultimate physiological and pathological actions and medicinal effects which lie at the very foundation of all healthy, diseased and curative processes.

RESUMÉ.—The following is a brief summary of the facts and inferences which appear to be indicated by the foregoing investigations.

1st.—That the disease occurring near Lancaster, Ohio, here described, and which proved so fatal, is *Angina Maligna*.

2nd.—That *Angina Maligna* is a contagious disease.

3rd.—That *Angina Maligna* is closely allied to *Scarlatina Anginosa* and that diphtheritic diseases generally are allied to those of the scarlatina type.

4th.—That the primary seat of the disease in both scarlatina and diphtheria is the epithelial cells. That these are so deranged in their functions by the morbific cause of the disease, that the nutrient products which they organize become so poisoned that they poison the tissues they are designed to nourish. This poisoning takes place during the period of incubation.

5th.—That morbific poisons cannot enter the system without first passing through and primarily deranging the epithelial cells and their products; as these cells envelop the entire organism, and guard all the approaches to it. That they affect the tissues by poisoning the organized matters which go to their support.

6th.—That the epithelial cells of mucous and serous surfaces assimilate and organize all the nutrient matters which go to build up and support the tissues.

7th.—That the perceptible symptoms of these diseases are but expressions of the efforts of nature to eliminate from the system the morbific poison.

8th.—That the exudations of the mucous surfaces in diphtheria are produced by the too rapid metamorphosis of mucous cells into filaments, which filaments become woven together, forming a felt-like membrane, before they are fully liberated from the follicles.

9th.—That the tendency to filament metamorphosis in diphtheria is general throughout the epithelial system, showing that it is a systemic disease.

10th.—That the *Mucor Malignans* appears to be the primary cause of *Angina Maligna*, and of *Angina Membranacea*. That the diseases are specifically the same, the difference being caused by the state of the system in the person attacked.

11th. That as the tendency is for the cells to become developed into filaments and resultant membranes before they are fairly out of the follicles, the object of any treatment should be to retard this filamentous development and promote the secretions, so that the cells may escape before they become filaments, also to check the development and to destroy the fungoid cause.

12th.—When the filaments are strong and membranes tough and adhesive, mercurials should be resorted to, to soften the threads and render exudation less adhesive.

13th.— That these diseases are but the efforts of nature to eradicate from the system morbific matters, that it should be the constant care of the physician not to run counter to nature in the efforts to cure the vitiated condition of the organism, but simply to endeavor to destroy the cause, and so to equalize, aid and modify her actions as to alleviate suffering, facilitate her processes, and guard against dangerous results.

14th.—That it is a normal action for the cell products of epithelial cells to become gradually metamorphosed into filaments.

15th.—That if by any cause the metamorphosis prematurely commences and the process is accelerated, it becomes a pathological action, which tends to result in grave abnormal conditions. In epithelial tissue there result membranes, exudations, and clots; in connective tissue, the various cancerous and fibrous growths.

16th.—That the epithelial cells have a life independent of the animal, all the external and internal surfaces of which they envelope and protect.

17th.—That they appear to be the primary seat of the functional derangements in all true fevers.

18th.—That they are the probable organisms which receive the protective immunity by one attack of certain contagious diseases that tends to guard the system against a second invasion of the same.

19th.—That in health it would seem that neither nutrient, medicinal nor morbific agents can enter the system so as to nourish, medicate or vitiate the tissues of the organism, without first passing through the cells, and imparting a primary influence to them and the products they organize.

20th.—That it is probable that morbific matters poison the tissues of the body through the nutrient products organized for their support by the epithelial cells.

21st.—That local fever of the mucous surfaces may be excited at will by exposing them for a few minutes to contact with the

32 West 26th St., June, 1882.

spores of certain algæ and fungi that develope upon ague bogs, old straw, &c.

22nd.—That it is probable that by continued exposure to these and similar causes (the taking of spores into the system through the food eaten and the air inhaled), that febrile action over the entire epithelial surfaces, including those of the lacteal and lymphatic systems, would be excited, in which case general fever would result.

23d.—That the altion of the "*fever poison*" upon the nervous system is through the nutrient nerve products organized by the vitiated and functionally deranged epithelial cells, and hence is a secondary process or manifest symptom of the primary functional derangements of these epithelial cell organisms, or of the ultimate disease.

24th.—That the treatment should be *prompt and direct*, aimed not only at the destruction of the cause, but at the removal of all the pathological conditions and states which this cause has excited.

The *Mucor Malignans* should be checked in its development and destroyed, and at the same time the toughness and adhesiveness of the exudations should be softened, the choking and suffocation should be relieved, and the throat, fauces and air passages be kept in as comfortable a state as possible. To destroy the cause, quinia sulphate—all things considered—is the best and most reliable remedy, as it braces up the enfeebled system while it is destroying the fungus.

It is not enough to give it every two hours or every hour, but it should be administered every half hour, and in some instances perhaps even oftener. It should be given in powder, so as to keep the throat and fauces constantly covered with it, and if necessary it should be snuffed and inhaled into the air passages. To destroy the toughness of the filaments and the adhesiveness of the membranes, small doses of mercurial often repeated are useful. To relieve the choking and suffocation, the simple hop poultice, applied as hot as it can be borne around the neck, and so covered as to allow the steam from it to be inhaled, is a very effectual relief. Also small doses of sulphuric ether in coffee, or the inhaling of a few drops of nitrate of amyl, may prevent sudden suffocation in cases where the physician is called in the last stages, and through these precious time may be gained for using vigorously the quinine.

In conclusion, I take pleasure in expressing my obligations to Drs. Boestler, Effinger and Lewis, who have felt interest in my labors, and to whom I am indebted for much excellent material in these examinations.

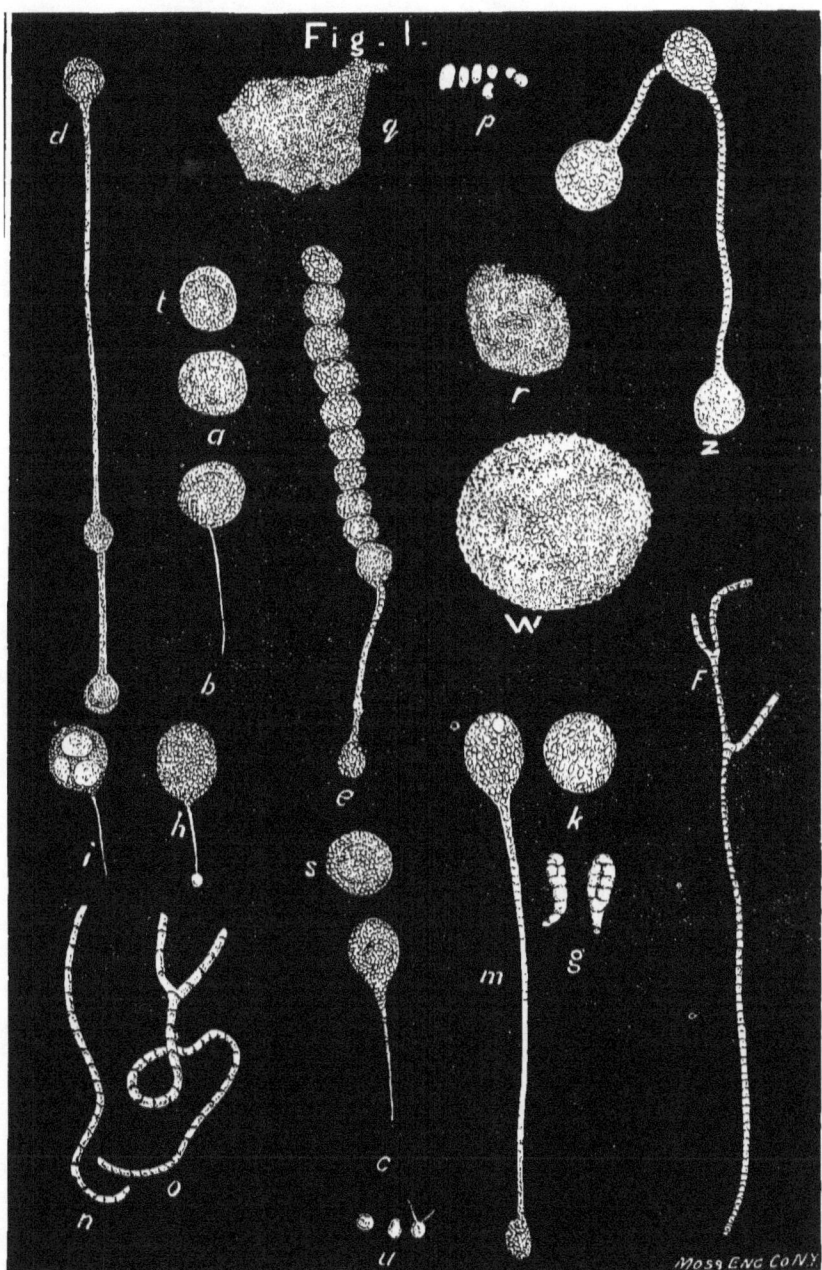

Fig. 1.

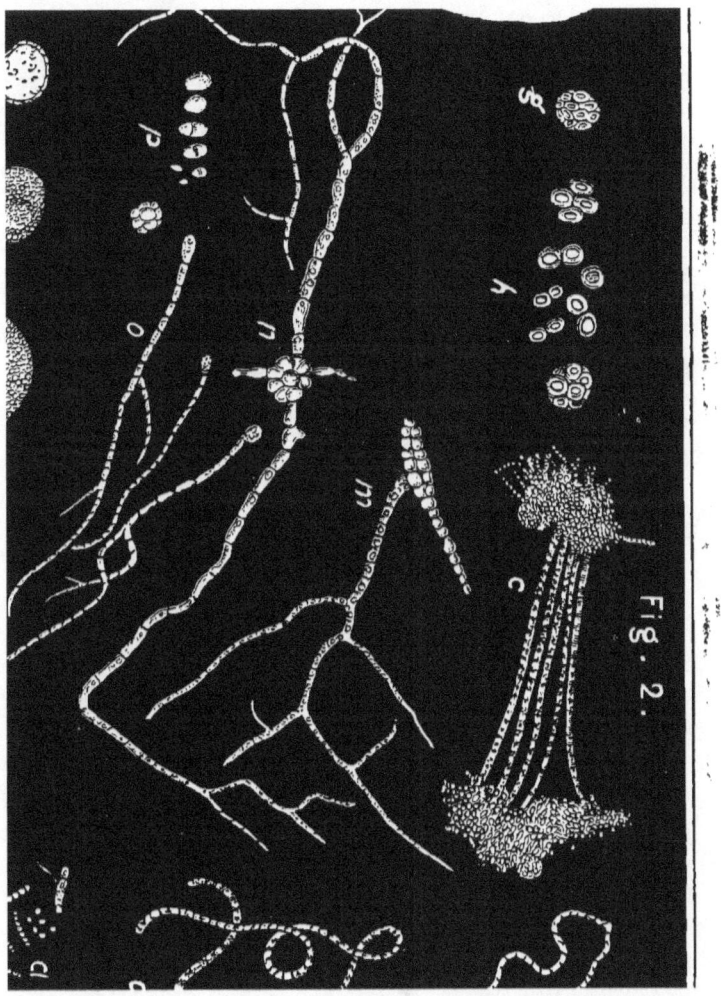

Fig. 2.

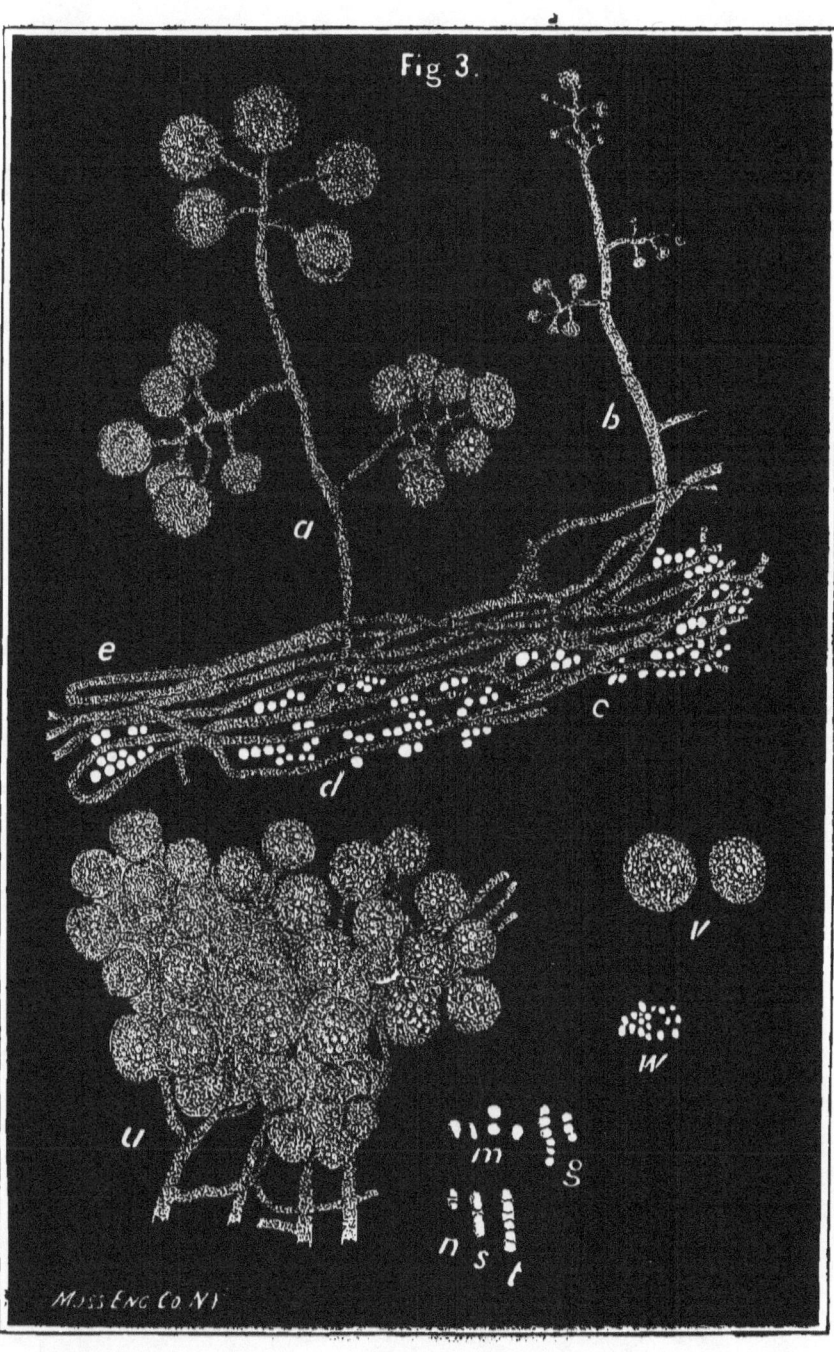

Fig 3.

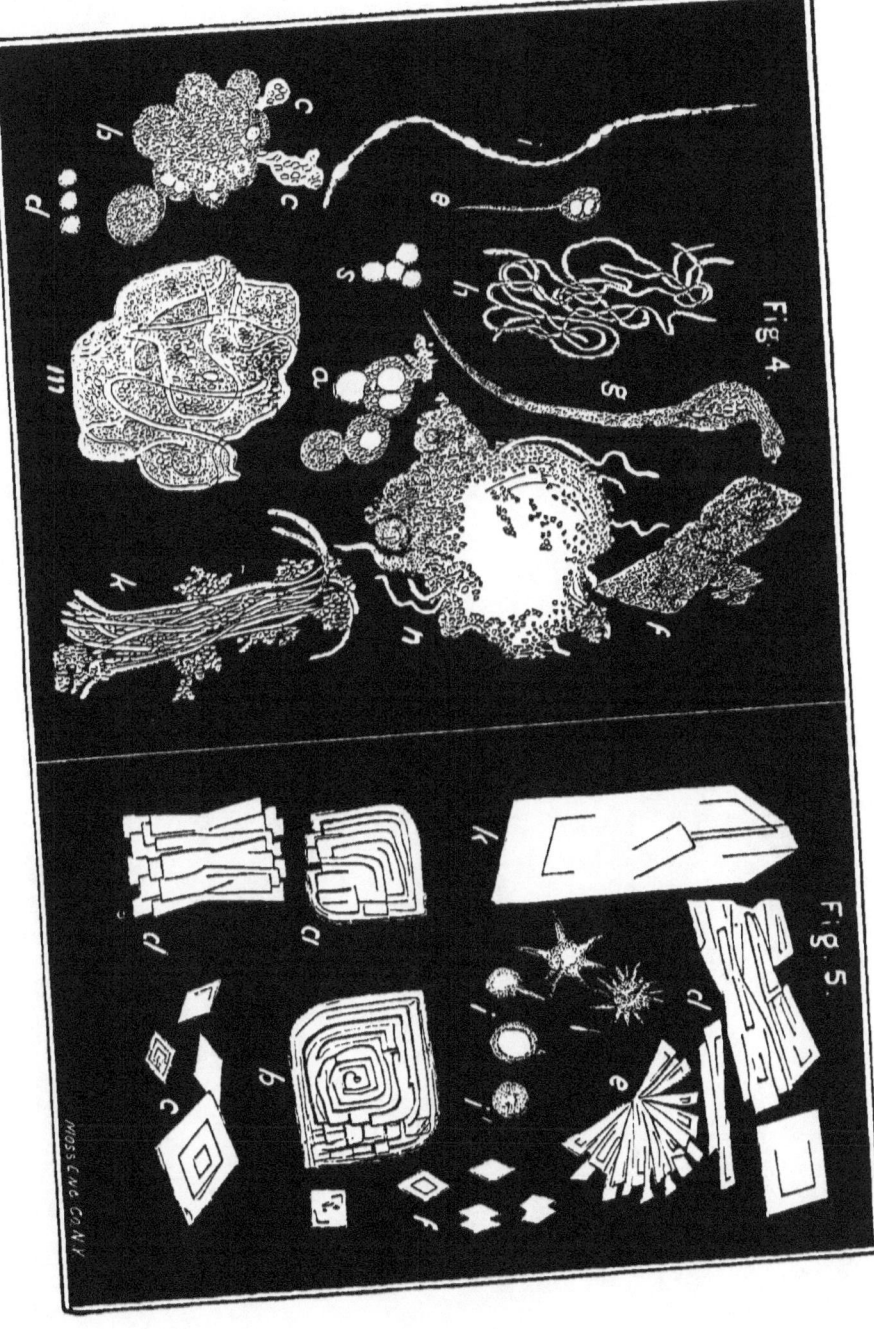

Fig. 4.

Fig. 5.

MOSS ENG CO.N.Y.

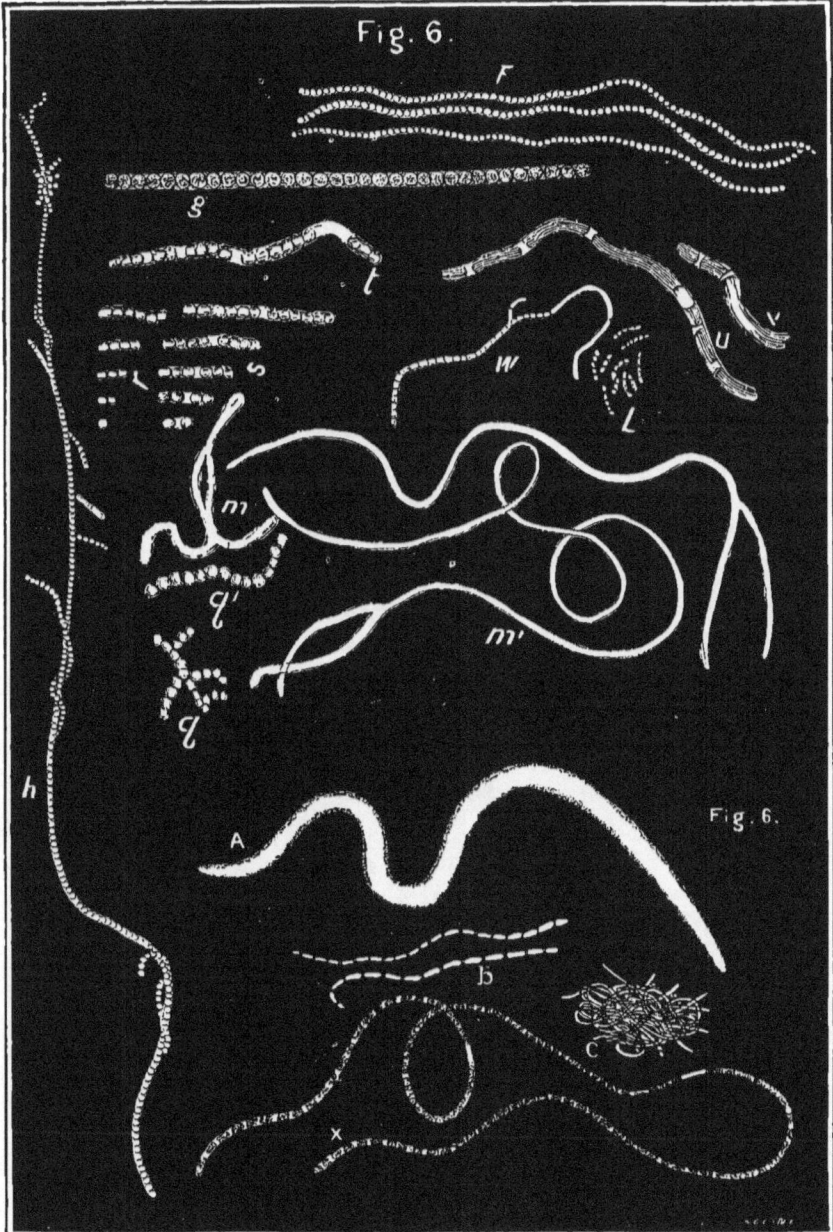

Fig. 6.

Fig. 7.

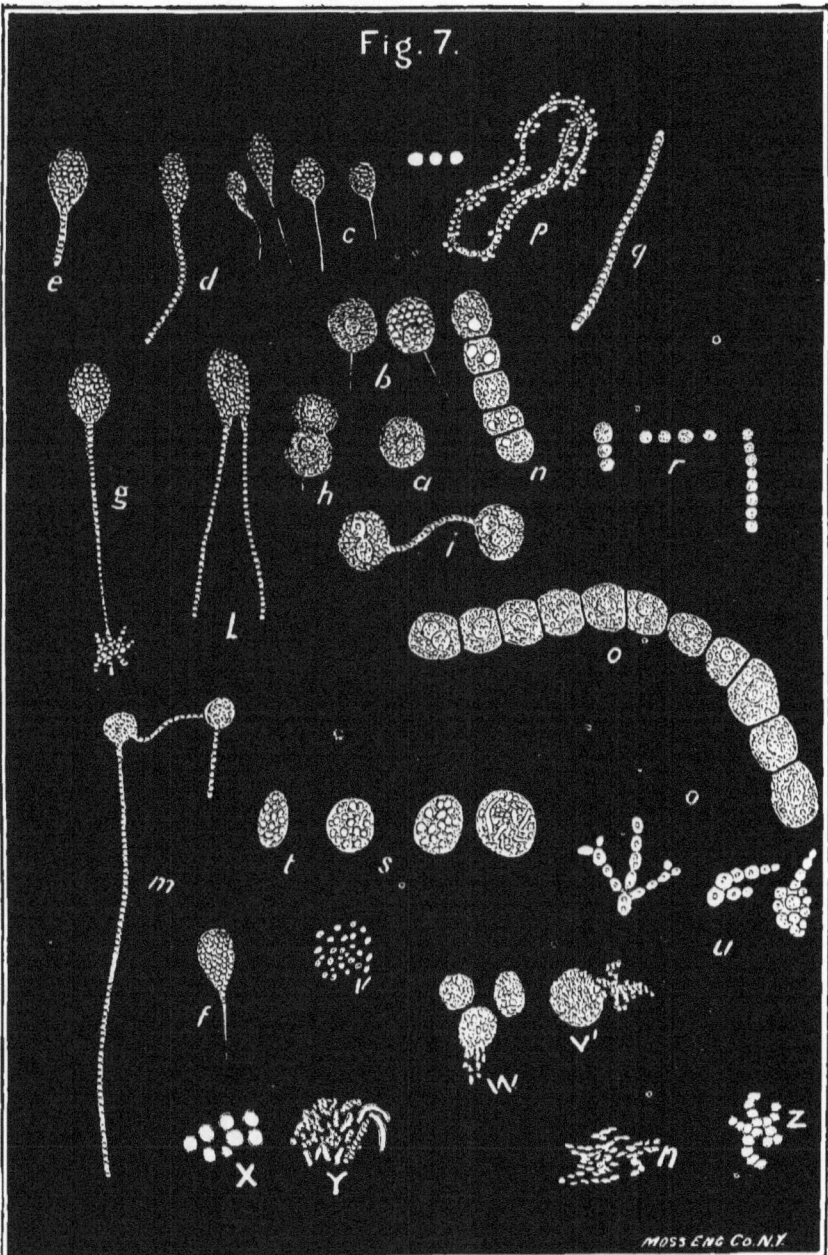

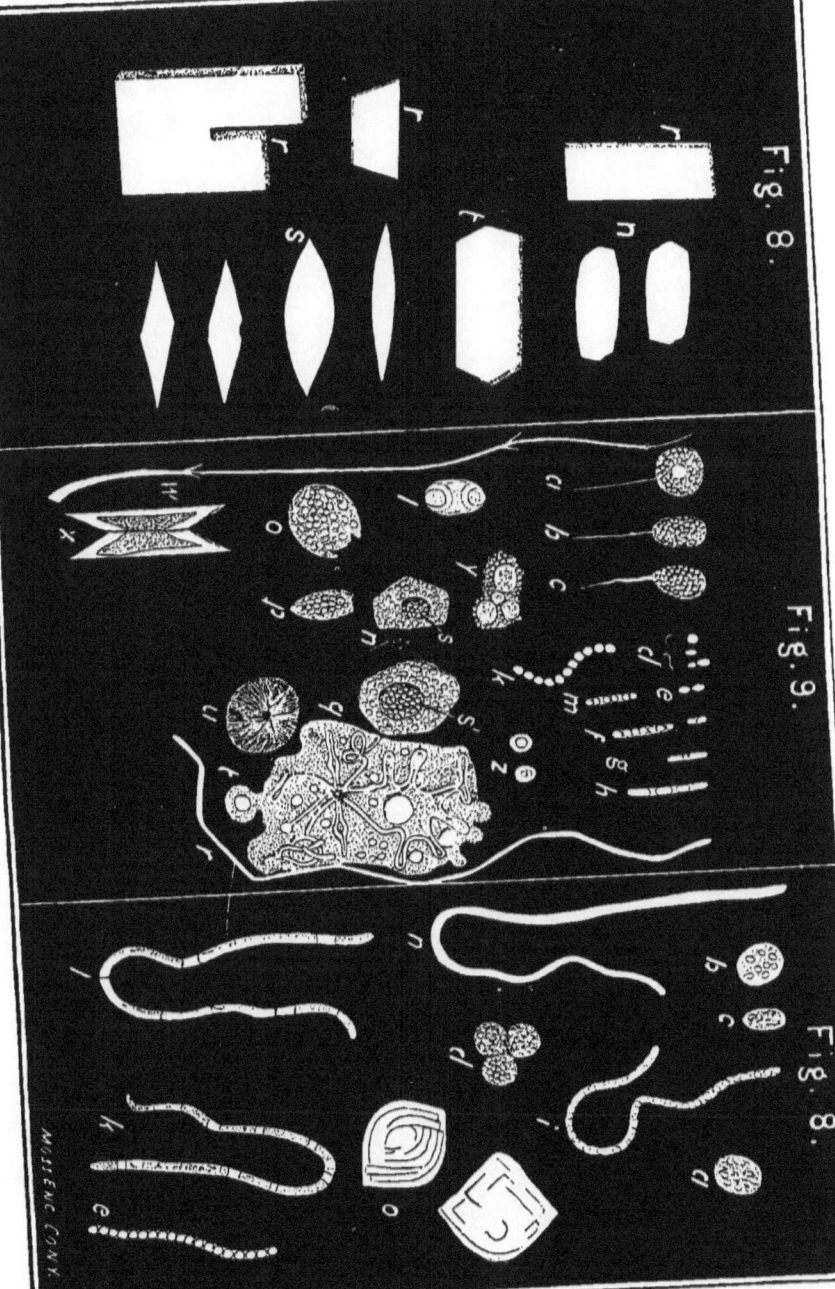

Fig. 8.

Fig. 9.

Fig. 8.

MÜLLENC CONX.

DESCRIPTION OF PLATES.

Amplification 2500 diameters and over.

PLATE 1ST. Forms found in the expectoration and exudations of diphtheria. A-S-T — Healthy buccal mucous corpuscles—page 409. B-C-H-I — Mucous corpuscles from Amos Bear's mouth, showing the spinning of filaments in diphtheria. D-E-M—Mucous cells connected with filaments. E—A row of mucous cells. F--mucous cells spun into a long branched filament. G.—Sporangia of sphærotheca pyrus—found also in pear blight. H-I-K-M-N-O—Mucous cells from Nancy Bear. U--Automobile microspores—the bacteria and micrococci of authors. P-Microspores found in Q and R. Q-R—Membrane in diphtheria. W-Membranous vegetable sac found in urine of scarlet fever, placed here for convenience. Z—Three cells in active filamentation.

PLATE 2D. FIG. 2. Bodies found in the sloughs of Amos Bear. Diphtheria. A—Embryonal form of vegetation—the bacteria and micrococci of writers—page 410. B-C-D—Mature mycelial filaments, running in all directions through the sloughs. E-F-G-H—Spores and microspores of the mucor malignans. I—Ascus. K-P—Spores of apple blight — sphærotheca pyrus. M-N-O—Spores with mycelial filaments do. U-V-W—Large mucous cells with entophytic fungi.

PLATE 3. FIG. 3.—The mature plant of diphtheria developed by culture.—page 411.

MUCOR MALIGNANS.—A-Fertile plant of Mucor Malignans with three clusters of sporangia. B—Plant with erect filament and undeveloped fruit. C-D-E—Stroma or membranous net work of mycelial filaments dotted over with microspores. W—Microspores that fill the sporangia at A. G-M-N-S-T—Automobile spores, some arranged into filaments. U—Collection of mature sporangia and filaments matted together as in the membrane. V—Separate mature sporangia.

PLATE 4. FIG. 4.—Abnormal morphological elements found in the blood of diphtheria and scarlet fever. A-B—Masses of colorless corpuscles filled with embryonal forms (spores) of the mucor malignans. C-C—Amœboid projections of protoplasm do do. D—Automobile microspores more highly magnified. E—Caudate cells like I and B, Fig. 1, Pl. 1. F—Endothelia of blood vessel with entophytal vegetation escaping. G—Colorless corpuscles forming into a filament. H and K—Skeins of mycelial filaments in the blood. M-N—Fibrin masses enclosing mycelial filaments. I—Filament resembling neurine—page 413.

FIG. 5.—Crystalline bodies found in the blood of scarlet fever and diphtheria. A-B-C-D—Uric acid. E-K—Peculiar forms do. I—Urates of soda and ammonium.

FIG. 6. PLATE 5.—Forms found in urine and sputa of scarlet fever and diphtheria. B—Mycelial filaments found in sputa of diphtheria. F-G—Filaments from urine of scarlet fever. H - R—Leptothrix with anabaina. M& M[1]—Structureless mycelial filaments—urine of diphtheria. A—Anguillila aceti from vinegar gargle of Amos Bear. Q-Q[1]—Cells uniting to form filaments. C—A knot of mycelial filaments such as are found scattered over the membranes of angina malignans. L-S-T-U-V-W—Embryonal spores and filaments more highly magnified.—The bacteria and micrococci of authors. X—Mycelial filaments such as also occurred in vast numbers in ripe persimmons in Ohio, 1862.

PLATE 6. FIG. 7.—Bodies found in the excretions of scarlet fever. A—Normal mucous cell. B-C-H—Mucous cells (scarlet fever), in an active state. D-E-L-M-I—Do. Do. in active filamentation. See also Z, Fig. 1. Plate 1. G—Mucous cell with micrococcus spores escaping at end of filament. N-O-near A—Do. Do. arranging themselves into rows to form filaments. P-Q—Mycelial filaments of mucor malignans. R—Moniliform filaments formed and forming. S & T--Highly refractive spheroidal cells of reddish orange colored filaments in cell on right. U—Alcholic yeast. V-V¹-W—Cells shedding contents. V-X-Y-Z-N near Z—Contents more highly magnified.

PLATE 7, FIG. 8.—Bodies found in urine of scarlet fever. A, B, C, sporangia of mucor malignans. D, parent epithelial cells from bladder. E, mycelial filament, I, K, L, N, near B, species of hypheothrix. O, uric acid. R, R, R, creatine. S, T, U, (N should be U) other forms of uric acid.

FIG. 9.—Scarlet fever. A, B, C, dermal epithelia cultivated. D, micrococcus spores from epithelium. E, F, K, ditto, united in moniliform filaments. G, H, ditto, united by twos and threes. L, diatom from drinking water. M, filament of spores united by twos. N, Q, Epithelial cells of skin of scarlet fever. O, P, abnormal sporangia of mucor malignans, both broken. R, long tubular mycelial filament. All these were automobile like oscillatoriacae. S, S, central nuclei of N and Q. T, patch of membrane with mycelial filaments of mucor malignans curiously twisted together and curled. U, urate of soda. W, barb of feather. X, phosphate of lime. Y patch of membrane.

www.ingramcontent.com/pod-product-compliance
Lightning Source LLC
Chambersburg PA
CBHW030912260626
47169CB00008B/2803